OPERATION STALAG

Late in 1942 Dutch Underground agents
delivered to British Intelligence an insane
young RAF pilot – the sole survivor of fifty
others from Stalag IIIB, all shot in cold
blood – but by whom and for what reason?
Churchill suspected a massive blackmail
threat involving 100,000 Allied POWs in
German camps, which could put an end to
the invasion of Europe. So British
Intelligence ordered its crack commando
squad, The Destroyers, into action. Under
the leadership of ruthless, one-eyed
Lieutenant Crooke, V.C., they set off on a
dangerous mission into Nazi Germany to
find the unknown Gestapo killer.

OPERATION STALAG

OPERATION STALAG

by

Charles Whiting

Dales Large Print Books
Long Preston, North Yorkshire,
BD23 4ND, England.

British Library Cataloguing in Publication Data.

Whiting, Charles
    Operation Stalag.

    A catalogue record of this book is
    available from the British Library

    ISBN   1-84262-284-6 pbk

First published in Great Britain in 1975 by
Seeling Service & Co.

Cover illustration by arrangement with G.B. Print Ltd.

The moral right of the author has been asserted

Published in Large Print 2004 by arrangement with
Eskdale Publishing

Dales Large Print is an imprint of Library Magna Books Ltd.

Printed and bound in Great Britain by
T.J. (International) Ltd., Cornwall, PL28 8RW

THE DESTROYERS:
OPERATION STALAG

STALAG: n. German prison camp, esp. for non-commissioned officers and men

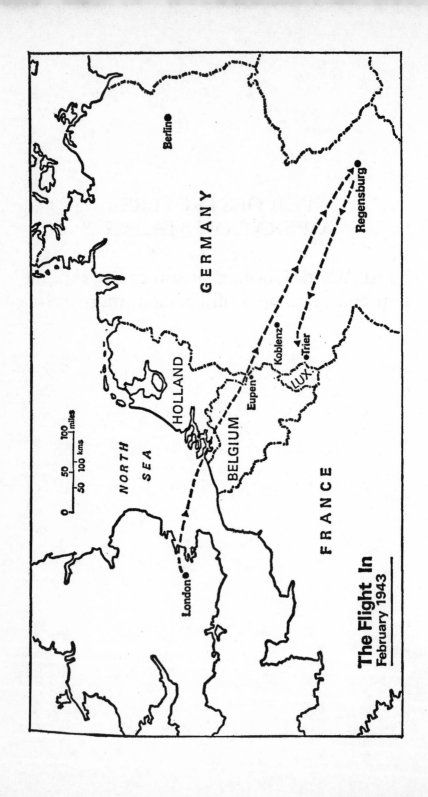

The Flight In
February 1943

The Destroyers' escape from Stalag Luft VIIb

February 1943

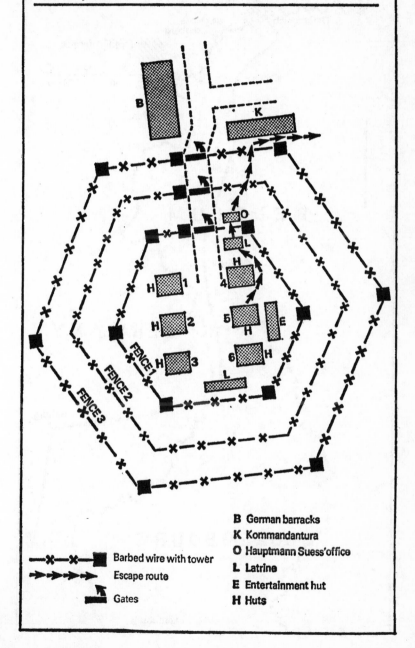

B German barracks
K Kommandantura
O Hauptmann Suess' office
L Latrine
E Entertainment hut
H Huts

─×─×─ ■ Barbed wire with tower
▶▶▶▶ Escape route
▐ Gates

SECTION ONE: THE WAY IN

'Mallory, it's up to your Destroyers to save D-Day.'

'C' Head of M.I.6 to Commander Mallory,
Feb. 1943.

1

'*Nicht schlagen!*'

The horrified shriek came echoing down the long, white-tiled corridor of the mental diseases wing. The two elegantly-tailored Royal Navy officers looked at the grey-haired RAMC Brigadier, an unspoken question in their eyes. The Brigadier, once one of Harley Street's most eminent consultants, avoided their looks.

They marched on down the corridor of the 80th General Military Hospital. Three men in light blue hospital pyjamas, accompanied by a corporal in whites, shuffled by, their eyes blank and staring. As the terrible scream rang out again, they did not even blink. 'My God,' said Admiral Godfrey, head of Naval Intelligence, 'who's that? A German POW?' The Brigadier shook his head. 'I'm afraid not, gentlemen,' he said. 'I wish in a way he were. No, he's one of our boys.' The screaming came closer. '*Nicht schlagen! Nicht schlagen!*' It echoed down the corridor and made Commander Mallory's

13

hair stand up on the nape of his neck. He shivered and whispered to Admiral Godfrey, 'It means "don't hit me", Admiral.'

By the door from which the shrieks were coming a hatchet-faced redcap came to attention. His foot stamped down as he swung up a smart salute. But the suspicious look in his eyes did not relax. 'Can I see your identity cards, gentlemen?' he asked.

'You know me, Corporal!' the Brigadier snapped. 'I've been here every day this week.'

'Your card, sir, if you don't mind,' the MP said unemotionally. As he examined their passes, Mallory saw that his hand was close to his service revolver. The call from Number Ten which had sent them speeding out of London two hours before had clearly not been for nothing; this was definitely something big!

Satisfied, the MP knocked on the door. It opened to reveal a big orderly with close cropped hair and a bulge which indicated a revolver under his white overall. 'All right, Charlie, they can go through,' the MP said.

'This way, gentlemen,' the orderly said.

Definitely Field Security, Mallory thought. They passed through.

The man they had come to see was pressed with his arched back against the metal frame

14

of the Army bed, his upper body rigid, his wolfish face hollowed-out and emaciated with pain and undernourishment. There were flecks of spittle at the corners of his mangled bitten lips, from which fresh blood was dripping on to the white sheets. A mad red light burned in the man's eyes. Both his hands were shackled to the bed, rubber wrapped around the metal.

'A safety precaution,' the Brigadier explained, following the direction of their horrified gaze. He nodded to a swarthy little man in the uniform of a captain in the RAMC, a hypodermic in his hand. 'Captain Maier, who is in charge of the case.'

The doctor gave a strange little continental bow from the waist.

'Perhaps you can explain, Maier,' the Brigadier said. Maier had a slight foreign accent; perhaps one of those Austrian doctors who had flooded into Britain in 1938 when Hitler occupied their country and started persecuting the Jews. He pointed to the man on the bed, whose lips moved ceaselessly as if he were carrying on a conversation with someone, yet whose eyes remained blank and unseeing. 'The patient escaped from Stalag Luft Three in Poland a month ago. From what little

15

identification he still had on him when the Moonlight Squadron of the RAF picked him up from the Dutch partisans last week, we learned that he is a former pilot, Flying Officer...'

'There's no need to give a name,' Brigadier Patton interrupted hastily. He turned to the Admiral. 'The powers that be don't want it known – even to you.'

Mallory looked at his chief. Admiral Godfrey, the man who had done so much to make an effective organization out of Naval Intelligence over the past three years, said nothing; but there was a light in his eyes which indicated that there would be a few sharp words said the next time he met his colleagues in Joint Intelligence.

The doctor continued. 'The Dutch section of the SOE* arranged the operation. It went off without a hitch, save for one thing. The poor man's mind has gone – gone completely.'

He looked down at the human wreck stretched out on the bed.

'I have worked on him for a week now – to

*Special Operations Executive, sabotage and spy organization set up on Mr Churchill's suggestion in 1940.

no avail.' He looked at the three officers. 'Something so terrible happened to him that his subconscious has deliberately censored it from his mind. Now all the mental power left to him concerns itself with defence – defence against pain.'

'Why, Doctor?' Mallory broke the silence.

'Let me show you something first,' Maier replied.

He turned to the tortured figure on the bed, whose right fist was tightly clenched over something. '*Sie*,' he snapped in a parody of some Prussian officer on the parade ground, '*was machen Sie, Kerl?*'

The reaction was horrifying. The man jerked back as if he had suddenly been given an electric shock. His eyes were filled with fear. '*Nein, nein!*' he screamed, tearing at the steel bands fastening his hands to the bed. '*Nicht schlagen, nicht schlagen!*'

Mallory shuddered. The man was fighting the shackles like a trapped animal, his eyes bulging, froth gathering at his lips, his body writhing from side to side, as if he were trying to escape from something.

'All right,' the Brigadier said. 'Thank you for the demonstration, Maier. That's enough.'

The little Captain nodded. Soothingly he

17

put his pudgy hand on the man's sweat-lathered brow. The pilot continued to writhe, but he kept his hand there, whispering gently: *'Schon gut; schon gut; wir tun dir nichts.'*

The words had their effect. The pilot relaxed. The crazy light fled from his eyes. The harsh, hectic breathing stopped. The energy of madness drained from him and he lay there motionless and apathetic once again.

The Admiral shook his head. There were tears in his eyes. He turned to the Brigadier. 'My God, Patton, what happened to the poor chap?' he asked. 'Those hands, for instance.' He pointed to the pilot's scarred left hand.

'His nails have been pulled off – forcibly,' the Brigadier said gruffly. 'And look at this.' He walked over to the patient. The eyes did not even flicker.

Swiftly he undid his buttons and pulled aside the jacket. Mallory gave a gasp of horror. His chest was marked by a series of suppurating lacerations.

'The poor fellow has been whipped with a steel whip,' he explained. The pilot gave no sign that he was aware of the Brigadier. 'And they've done something else to him –

further down,' he added, without looking at them. 'Irreparable damage. He'll never have a love life.'

He stepped back and nodded to Maier. 'Yes, you can do it now. There is nothing more we can do.'

Maier held the hypodermic to the light. Then, turning to the man on the bed, he rolled up the sleeve of his left arm and pressed the needle home. The pilot went limp. His eyes rolled upwards and something dropped from his clenched right fist. Hastily Admiral Godfrey bent down to pick it up. Maier put down the hypodermic in the little kidney-shaped tray near the bed. His hand was trembling. He reached out his forefinger and thumb – and slowly but firmly closed the patient's eyes!

'A sedative?' Mallory asked in alarm.

'No,' the Brigadier said tonelessly, his gaze directed at his gleaming shoes, 'a terminal injection...'

Shaken by the legal murder they had just witnessed, the two Naval Intelligence men shook hands with the Brigadier. 'Goodbye, gentlemen,' he said, 'I've got to get back and make the necessary arrangements.'

Slowly and in silence the other two started

to crunch their way over the frozen gravel towards the waiting staff car. Across the fields came the thin high wail of the air-raid siren. Another tip-and-run raider, Mallory told himself. The Germans had been running in a lot of the new Focke-Wulf 190s this winter. The radial-engined fighter-bombers would come winging over the coast at 400 mph to shoot up one of the little coastal towns in the south-east and be away before Fighter Command could scramble their Spits. They rarely did any harm, but they served to remind the civilians that the war was still very far from won, in spite of the recent victories at El Alamein and Stalingrad.

As the ack-ack began to thump faintly in the distance, Mallory broke the silence. 'Did that really happen in there, Admiral?' he asked.

Godfrey stopped. 'Yes, it did, Miles – and on orders right from the top.'

Mallory could not repress his sense of outrage. He had been in Naval Intelligence for three years now, ever since Godfrey had taken him into the Naval Reserve, and he had undergone some shocks in that time, but never anything like this. 'But why? What had that poor chap done that he had to be done away with like a dog being put down?'

Godfrey took him by the arm. 'Before I answer your question, let me tell you something about that poor chap who just died in there. The Brigadier will later notify his relatives that he passed away due to enemy action – but not just yet. As you have already heard, the man escaped from a German POW camp. But he wasn't alone. There were another hundred officers who made the breakout with him. Naturally most of them knew they had no chance of making it back to the U.K. The camp's in Poland after all. But the prospect of getting out of the cage for a couple of days and the knowledge that they were upsetting the Hun was enough for most *kriegies,* as they call themselves. After all by getting the enemy to deploy a couple of infantry battalions to look for them, they were directly helping our war effort. But this time, things turned out differently. Normally, our sources in the camps – we have contact with most Stalags – report that the returned *kriegie* is put in solitary on bread and water for a couple of weeks after recapture. Sometimes he even gets beaten up by the guards. Unpleasant, but not fatal. However, this time not one of them returned to the camp – nor to any other camp that we have contact with. The only one we know anything definite about is that poor unfortunate back there, who somehow struggled through Germany until he crossed the frontier near Aachen – apparently it's the route we recommend to escapees. As you saw, he must have suffered the most hideous treatment to break down like that; and they'd emasculated him too. Perhaps it's better that he went like that.'

The Director of Naval Intelligence crooked his finger and clicked it back and forth, as if he were pulling a trigger. 'Joint Intelligence thinks that the Hun shot the others,' he said simply.

'Good God!'

'Yes,' Godfrey said solemnly, 'that poor man up there was the sole survivor. That was why he was so important. We even risked one of the Moonlight Squadron's planes to pick him up. That's the first time we have ever done that for an escaped POW.'

'Then why kill him?' Mallory asked.

'There were several reasons. The first is naturally humanitarian. The poor chap would have been a vegetable for the rest of his life, even if he had been able to survive his injuries. The second is morale. Our bomber crews have been taking a terrible beating ever since Bomber* began the mass raids. If they had learned what might happen to them on capture...' He left the sentence unfinished. 'You understand, I'm sure.'

Mallory nodded.

'The third reason is that we don't want the Germans to know that a survivor reached us.'

'And the fourth?'

Admiral Godfrey pursed his lips. 'I think on consideration, Miles, that I shall leave that one to C.'

*Sir Arthur Harris, head of Bomber Command and nicknamed 'Bomber'.

2

Camille, the Niçois waiter who always
served Mallory at Frascati's Restaurant
beamed when he saw his favourite client
follow Admiral Godfrey into the Edwardian
dining-room. 'Ah, good day, Commander,'
he said in his fractured English, rubbing his
hands together as if he were already savouring the fat tip which the wealthy ex-banker
usually gave him, 'I have something very
special for you this day – mushromps on
toast.'

Mallory forced a smile. *'Mushrooms,*
Camille,' he corrected him, but he couldn't
forget the scene in the Military Hospital
that morning.

'Yes,' Camille said, 'mushromps!'

Mallory gave up. He followed the Admiral
to where C was seated on one of the
restaurant's plush chairs under a gilded
Edwardian cherub, staring moodily out of
the window. The head of British Secret
Intelligence nodded curtly to them, muttered a barely polite 'Afternoon,' and added,

25

'Let's get the ordering done with. There's never anything on the menu these days except those damned dried eggs and something repulsive called snoek.' While the two senior officers busied themselves with the big menu cards, which promised a lot and yielded little, Mallory studied C out of the corner of his eye.

Mallory knew C's background. It was utterly conventional: Eton, the Guards, World War I with the usual DSO and MC; thereafter intelligence work until in the first months of the war he had taken over the SIS. In other words, a typical regular officer with perhaps somewhat limited intellectual power. Yet, watching him as he bent over the menu, Mallory saw that there was something different about him – his eyes. They were cold and calculating, those of a man who regarded his fellow human beings as pawns to be dealt with and dispensed with when necessary. In short, C was a man to be feared.

When the waiter had taken their order, C opened the conversation. 'Good security here,' he said, 'plenty of space between the tables. Not packed in like a lot of sardines. And of course, only the very best people eat here.'

Admiral Godfrey flashed Mallory a

warning look. The Commander caught himself in time. In his three years with Naval Intelligence he had met several of the 'very best people' who would betray their country at the drop of a hat.

C turned to him. 'Commander, are you a bigot?'

'A bigot, sir?' Mallory asked, startled. 'Well I have my prejudices. I don't like professional Irishmen and people who wear their fountain pens in their breast pockets and–'

C held up his thin pale hand to stop the flow of words. 'Not that kind of bigot, Commander.' He smiled but there was no answering light in his eyes. 'You'd better tell him, Godfrey.'

The Admiral explained. 'There are perhaps a thousand people in this country today…'

'Thirteen hundred to be precise,' C interrupted.

'Thank you. Well, thirteen hundred, who know when the Second Front will start – the invasion of Europe. These people are code-named "Bigot".'

'Oh, I see,' Mallory said, suddenly realizing that he was on the fringe of one of the greatest secrets of the war.

C gave Godfrey an almost imperceptible nod.

'All right, Miles, I'm now going to make you a bigot too.' He hesitated, as if he did not want to even utter the word aloud. In the background Camille was hissing a stream of Niçois curses at a slow assistant waiter. 'The invasion will be launched in April, 1944, roughly one year from now.'

'That's very good of you, Admiral,' Mallory said, suddenly aware he was one of the élite; even the Monarch did not know the date. 'But why the honour?'

C answered his question. 'Because, Commander, that second front may never take place!' His pale face was suddenly taut and pinched. Mallory could see the worried wrinkles increase around his cold eyes. 'Yesterday evening after we discovered that Brigadier Patton and that foreign doctor of his could get nothing out of their patient, the PM held an emergency meeting of the cabinet. I was privileged to attend. The PM, as you might know, is a very moody man – a very difficult one. But he is a very brilliant man too. He saw the problem immediately I explained that one hundred of our POWs had disappeared during an attempted escape and were presumed dead. You see, Commander, at present there are some two hundred thousand Allied prisoners of war in

Europe. They are mostly British, but there are quite a few Americans too since North Africa. They are green of course, they must learn the hard way.'

C lowered his voice slightly. 'Imagine what would happen if the boche decided on the first day we invaded Europe to start executing these prisoners publicly? One thousand the first day – two thousand the second, ten thousand the third.' Mallory saw immediately what he meant. Although Britain had thousands of German POWs, public opinion would not allow them to be slaughtered in retaliation. 'It would hold up the decision to push on inland once we had secured the beaches?'

'Not *hold up, cripple!* It would cripple the operation completely.'

There was silence as the three men mulled over the full implications of his statement.

C cleared his throat. 'The PM saw the answer immediately. There are those who say he is an eighteenth-century man. That may be so, but he is well attuned to the unpleasant aspects of our own century. It is clear, as he told me personally after the cabinet meeting, that after the disappearance of our POWs last month the Germans hold a trump card in their hands.'

'An unprecedented kind of blackmail on a gigantic scale,' Admiral Godfrey said.

'Yes, and we must do something about it *now* – before it is too late. Mallory,' he turned to the Commander. 'I believe you have a little group of men under your command at the DNI who have – let us say – few inhibitions?'

'You mean the Destroyers, sir?'

C nodded.

'Yes, they are men without inhibitions,' he said and added thoughtfully. 'You might call them men who are licensed to kill.' For the first time he used the phrase that he would one day make world-famous.

'You might tell me a little about them,' C said, taking up his glass and looking over its edge at him.

'Well, last year the DNI was given the job of preventing the Chief-of-Staff of the Egyptian Army doing a bunk to the Germans and helping Rommel to raise a revolution in the Egyptian Army behind Montgomery's back. It was just before Alamein. Montgomery was scraping the barrel for manpower so I had to find my own men for the task.'

'Where?'

'In the glasshouse,' Godfrey interrupted with a laugh. 'Go on, Miles, tell him.'

'That's right; in the Cairo Military Prison,

together with Second Lieutenant Crooke.'

C put down his glass at the mention of the name. 'You mean the chap who won the Victoria Cross trying to kill Rommel and then got almost cashiered because he struck the Deputy Commander, Home Forces?'

Mallory repressed a grin at the look of alarm on C's face; obviously he shared the rest of the Regular Army's prejudice against the one-eyed second lieutenant who was determined to follow his own lone star, even to the extent of striking the pompous Deputy Commander, Home Forces when the latter had refused to send him overseas again to an active posting in his beloved desert. 'Yes that's the one. Well, together we picked five men from the glasshouse. The scum of the British Army, but each one in his way a brave man and an expert in spite of – in some cases – crime sheets as long as one's arm.'

Camille was approaching, silver tray held high, his swarthy face beaming proudly, as he bore his 'mushromps on toast' towards them.

'Are they killers?' C asked hastily while the waiter was still out of earshot.

'Yes, one might say that,' Mallory answered.

'Good, because I need men who are

31

prepared to kill in the most brutal way. I need them to kill one man and to do it soon.'

'Who?'

Godfrey answered for C. He took out of his pocket the object he had picked up from the floor in the bare hospital room, after it had dropped from the dying pilot's fingers. 'The man who owned this.'

Mallory stared at it in silence. It was a cheap round glass scent bottle bearing the picture of a horseman chalking a number on the wall of a house. Mallory vaguely remembered the stuff from his pre-war business trips to Germany.

'Commander, I want your Destroyers to eliminate the owner of that bauble in the most hideous manner possible. Why?' he answered the question before Mallory could pose it. 'Because the PM wants the Germans warned that anyone who dares even harm a hair of the head of one of our chaps will suffer a terrible death. In this way even if Hitler wanted to carry out his monstrous plan, he would find no one – even among his most fanatical followers – who would dare execute it for him.' He paused and let Mallory absorb the information. 'So it's up to your Destroyers to save D-Day.'

3

'Y-Track' Stevens had made a study of housewives in his two years on the barrow after his release from Borstal in 1935. The cunning little cockney, who had masqueraded as a colonel in the desert for eighteen months, complete with his own RASC unit, before he had been sentenced to the glasshouse for nine years, later to be released to Mallory's Destroyers, felt there were three types. The young newly-weds starry-eyed and ecstatic about their Toms and Jacks. In his book they were no good for 'a bit of the other'. Then there were the 'muvvers': proud if worn possessors of snotty-nosed kids, their lives and conversations full of Billy's measles and Maggie's torn knickers. They were no good either. Finally there were thirty-to-thirty-five-year-olds, with kids who were growing up. In the one wartime leave and the couple of months he had been 'on the trot' as a deserter after Dunkirk, before they sent him to Africa, they had been the type he had looked for.

They were easy, only too ready to 'get 'em down and have a bit'.

He'd spotted her immediately the night before as he entered the pub in the Tottenham Court Road. A bit of chatter, a couple of ports and lemon and she'd been telling him her life story. Old man in a munition factory out at Brentwood. Ten quid a week. Nice money, but you do get lonely when he's on night shift, don't you? *You do!* And you can't stay in every night listening to Itma or Garrison Theatre. Tommy Handley's all right, but you want something else now and again, don't you? *You do!* At eleven o'clock on the nail he had her naked in the matrimonial bed, going at it like a fiddler's elbow.

Now it was just after dawn. Through a V-shaped chink in the blackout curtain he could see the cold, unfriendly, winter light. He looked at his watch. Time he was going. Her old man's bus from Brentford would be coming in soon. Careful not to wake her, he slipped out of bed. His desert bronze, marred by the ugly red of the newly healed wound, was beginning to fade now. Swiftly he began to pull on his uniform. Turning he blew her a kiss and smiled cynically when he realized he had not even bothered to ask her name the night before in the pub. Now it didn't matter any more; he'd never see her again.

His heavy ammo boots in his hands, he crept downstairs in his stockinged feet. Outside there was the creak of the little gate. Tired feet were coming up the path. 'Time I went,' Stevens muttered to himself.

As the unknown fumbled with his latch-key, Stevens ran through her purse. Thirty bob. That'd pay for the two ports and lemon. As the door began to open, Stevens scooped a handful of cigarettes from the open box on the table and ran to the back door, which he had prudently asked about the night before.

The morning air was cold. He shivered and was about to set off down the street, when a harsh voice behind him snapped. 'You Stevens?'

He swung round.

Two military policemen were standing in the next doorway, their faces red with the cold. They were staring at his death's head unit patch, the insignia of the Destroyers.

'Yes,' Stevens said cockily, '*Private* Stevens, if you don't mind!'

The older of the redcaps glowered at him. 'Belt up,' he said. 'We've been waiting here for three hours while you've been knocking that off upstairs.'

'Just the warrior home from the wars enjoying his simple pleasures,' Stevens said, grinning at their discomfiture. 'You know how it is – take a long look at the floor my darling, 'cos you'll only be seeing the ceiling for the next three days.'

The MPs fell in on either side of him, dwarfing him with their greatcoated bulk.

He looked up at them in mock alarm. 'Don't tell me I'm for the nick again?'

'No, you're lucky this time,' the older man said surlily. 'Commander Mallory wants to see you back at his headquarters immediately. There's something on.'

Stevens' good mood vanished. He knew what that meant. Wordlessly he allowed himself to be escorted to the waiting 15-CWT truck.

It was typical mid-winter English weather. During the night it had tried to snow, but just before dawn the snow had turned to rain. Now although it was mid-morning, the grass was still wet and a light mist was beginning to descend upon the firing ranges. Up on his wooden-legged tower the range officer wondered whether he should not close the range for the day. Visibility was lousy and he doubted whether they'd even be able to see the target in fifteen minutes' time. But down below Lone Star Alamo Jones, known to the Destroyers as 'Yank', continued to fire. He lay flat on his belly, not noticing the wet earth, his legs wide apart in an inverted V. Adjusting the back sight of the Lee Enfield up to three hundred yards, he took careful aim.

Crack!

The bullet sped to its target while the recruits using the range that morning stared down at him and the other man firing against him. A moment later, the marker appeared on the target from the pit and indicated a bull.

The leather-faced 42-year-old Texan, who had been a soldier-of-fortune for the past seven years until his cold-blooded murder of a group of German POWs had brought him to the Cairo glasshouse, grunted with satisfaction. Six bulls out of six! He turned to the guardsman, who lay on the grass next to him. 'Okay, soldier, what are you going to do about that?' Peters, who looked every inch of what he had once been – a sergeant-major in the Guards – until his refusal to waste the lives of his men had brought him into the glasshouse – said nothing. He picked up the weapon he was trying out, the Lisle Silenced Carbine, and adjusted his position on the wet grass.

Peters felt the rifle as if it were an extension of himself, another arm. It was a beautiful weapon. If they ever went on ops again this was the weapon he would take. He breathed out very slowly. Very carefully, he squeezed the trigger. There was no answering crack. Just a barely audible plop. Behind him the crowd of recruits who happened to be witnesses to this strange duel strained their eyes to see the target. Even they knew that the carbine supposedly only had a range of two hundred metres – not much more than two hundred and twenty yards. A couple of moments, then the marker indicated that Peters had also scored six bulls.

'Hell's bells,' one of the recruits breathed in awe behind the two rivals. 'I'm glad you two buggers is on our side!' The Yank did not seem to hear. There was a slight flush on his lean yellow face. 'All right, you limey bastard,' he began, 'let's make it really difficult now. We'll sort the men from the boys…'

He never finished the sentence.

'You men there,' a voice called out.

The two marksmen looked round.

A full colonel in the Royal Artillery was coming towards them. Peters sprang to his feet and came to attention, as if he had just seen the Monarch himself. The Yank raised himself more slowly, a look of contempt on his face for the regular soldier who stood so rigidly at his side.

'I've just had a call from the Admiralty,' the Colonel said, his voice reflecting his bewilderment at why these two men should be so important. 'A staff car is coming to fetch you in fifteen minutes.' He consulted a slip of paper in his hand. 'You are to report to a Commander Mallory at once.' The guardsman said nothing.

The American breathed out hard. *'Christ on a crutch!* Not that business again!'

'And this is number one,
And I've got her on the run,
Lay me down, turn me round and do it
  again.
Roll me *over* in the clover. Roll me over and
  do it again...'

Gippo raised his thin voice above the off-key roar of the drunks and the tinkle of the piano. The pale-faced Americans were all eyes; they had long forgotten the drunks and the big-bosomed 'good-time girls' at the bar of the pub. Now he knew he had them in his hand. Gone were the days when he had been forced to sell pornographic photos of unusual happenings between donkeys and portly Arab ladies to wide-eyed tourists at Suez. Things were different now. He was a somebody, recognized for what he was – a British chap and undoubtedly the grandson of Field Marshal Kitchener, as his grandmother had always maintained, in spite of her lack of a wedding ring. 'Gentlemen,' he told them, his beady Levantine eyes sweeping the circle of innocent white faces, 'I would not do this, but I am wanting you to be our friends. You chaps are coming over here to help us and for this reason I am making this offer.'

He opened his skinny brown hand.

They gasped when they saw the brass buttons. 'Yes,' he said, savouring their awe, 'as I have been telling you, these are the buttons from the Desert Fox's uniform.'

'But say,' asked a fresh-faced young soldier, with the stripe of a Private First Class. 'How did you get them?'

Gippo raised his head in the Turkish

gesture of disbelief. 'That I am not permitted to say,' he said in his fractured English. He gave a quick look to left and right.

At the piano the drunken naval rating, with his cap stuck at the back of his head, had got up to 'Number Eight' and was doing something with 'her flue' before launching once again into his beery adventure 'in the clover'.

'Combined Operations,' he breathed. 'Top secret.'

'Gee.' The PFC was impressed. 'And you took them right off'n Rommel's own tunic?'

'Yes, and because we are friends, I'm going to let you each one of you buy just one. But only if you are promising me to be secret.'

'Sure, sure.' There was a murmur of assent from the GIs crowded round him.

Gippo grinned at them. Now all he had to do was to collect the money and be away. This was the third set of fools he had found since the pubs had opened that morning. If he rushed it, he could probably find another group before they closed. 'That will cost you one pound English,' he said hurriedly.

'How much is that, soldier?' the PFC asked. 'In greenbacks?'

Gippo did not know. Before the war at Suez, he had known the exchange rate of twenty important currencies. Now he was out of touch.

'Ten dollars,' he said hastily.

The PFC peeled off a ten-dollar bill and was about to hand it to him.

Gippo stretched out his skinny brown hand, but he never succeeded in taking the note. A firm white hand seized his own. He turned round to find himself looking into Commander Mallory's good-humoured face. 'So that's where the buttons of my second best uniform went to, eh Gippo?'

Behind the Commander there were two stony-faced petty officers of the Naval Police. 'It was just being a little joke, Captain, sir,' Gippo said.

Together the two petty officers went to Highgate Cemetery with Mallory and Gippo. Thaelmann, the German refugee, who was number five in the Destroyers, was where Gippo had said he would be: standing in silent devotion in front of the neglected tomb.

Mallory watched the Communist who had fled from a German concentration camp and had fought against his own country ever since. One day, he knew, Thaelmann would be a danger. At the moment he had need of him. 'Thaelmann,' he said.

The German spun round. He had been so absorbed in his contemplation of the weathered tomb that he had not heard them approach. His hand swung up and he gave Mallory a rigid salute.

Mallory respected Thaelmann. The torn ear and the bitter eyes were evidence of what he had gone through. Mallory pointed to the grave. 'One tends to forget that he died here in England. You'd think that the Soviet Embassy would look after the tomb more carefully.'

Thaelmann did not look round. 'Karl Marx was a great man, sir,' he said, 'but he would have been the last person to want a cult made of his memory. The Communist ideal is not the individual, but that of the people, all the people...'

Mallory held up his elegant, manicured hand to stop the unaccustomed flow of words. 'I know just what a delightful person he was,' he said cynically, 'but let us dispense with that now. There is a war to be won, you know.'

Mallory signalled the two petty officers to move back out of earshot. Then he said, 'Thaelmann, I'd like to ask you something. I want to know whether you would be prepared to go back to Germany with the Destroyers on a mission? Remember such an undertaking would be doubly dangerous for you, since you are a German and a wanted one.'

Thaelmann did not hesitate. 'Naturally, sir,' he said.

The Minister was one of the most powerful men in the kingdom and undoubtedly believed that he and his newspapers were the sole protectors of the British Empire. Now he listened in silence to the one-eyed subaltern. Silence was normally hard for him. He loved to talk. But he respected Crooke and did not interrupt.

'You must understand, sir, that there are corrupt forces at work – even in our own country – forces which can destroy the work of three hundred years if we don't do something to counter them. The British Empire could fall like that.' He snapped his fingers. 'If we don't take effective measures *now* to root out the traitors, the weak sisters, the appeasers – and dispense with them.'

The Minister was well aware just how dangerous Crooke was.

'Dispense with them' indeed; a polite euphemism for cold-blooded murder. After

44

Crooke, as the sole survivor of the abortive attempt to kill Rommel in 1942, had fought his way back through the desert with his eye shot out, it had been the Minister's newspapers which had run the campaign to make a hero out of him. It had been a dark period of the war and the country needed heroes. The result had been the award of the Victoria Cross. But the powers-that-be had underestimated Crooke, dominated by his ruthless drive to fight those forces at home and abroad which he felt were intent on bringing about the downfall of the British Empire. When the War Office had refused to send him overseas after his recovery, he had punched the Deputy Commander, Home Forces and narrowly avoided being cashiered.

'What do you mean by effective measures, Crooke?' the Minister asked.

'There are too many people in power, sir, who are still thinking in terms of the last war. Mass actions, involving hundreds of thousands of men who have been trained to carry out routine and predictable operations. Even the commandos have been taken over by the blimps and the office-seekers. What we need, sir, is a small group of professional, expert killers like my Destroyers. Men who have

45

nothing to lose and everything to gain – who will carry out the most ruthless actions, not only against military personnel but also civilians, because they know the only alternative is back to the military prison or its equivalent for years.'

The press lord shivered. The Lieutenant frightened him. He realized now that Crooke had come to see him to gain support for non-military operations. If the need arose, he wanted to use his Destroyers for political murders. 'I think I get you, Crooke,' he said, 'but where exactly do I fit into...' He never finished his question.

The red light on the intercom panel in front of him began to blink. A look of annoyance flashed across his face. He knew the call must be urgent. None of 'my nice young men from the posh public schools', as he called his aides, would otherwise dare to disturb him in conference. He leaned across the enormous desk, which served to emphasise his own tiny frame, and flicked the button. 'What is it?'

The fruity voice of his chief aide said, 'C, sir. C would like to speak to you.'

The Minister did not like C. He considered him self-important and inefficient, a typical product of the background and establishment which he hated even though he now belonged to it himself. But C had good contacts with the Palace and he knew if he were ever to become Prime Minister, he would have to retain the goodwill of the monarch. It would do no good to cross C. 'All right,' he said, 'put him on.'

He switched over to the scrambler and listened. Once he asked 'where' and a little later he objected 'Hasn't he been through enough?', but for the most part he listened in silence; again unusual for him with people he disliked.

'Thank you,' he said finally and put down the phone. For a moment or two he stared at Crooke in silence. Then he licked his lips and passed on the news. 'You're to go to the SOE headquarters in Baker Street,' he said. 'My chauffeur will take you. Commander Mallory will be waiting for you there.'

'My chief,' Crooke said, getting to his feet and reaching for his cap.

'Yes, I know. He's got another mission for you. I'll leave it up to Mallory to fill you in properly.'

Crooke put on his cap. His one eye gleamed. The Minister saw that the prospect of fresh blood-letting excited him intensely. 'Well, Crooke, there is nothing much for me to say, but good luck and happy landings.' He reached his hand across the desk, without attempting to get up.

'Thank you, sir. I hope you will bear in mind what I said and will try to help me when the time is opportune.'

'Of course you can rely on me, Crooke, and the organization I control.'

'Thank you, sir.'

As Crooke passed through the door, the Beaver bent down to his papers again. From what C had told him over the phone he would not see Crooke again.

4

It was two weeks later. At the window of the Baker Street house which was the SOE headquarters, Mallory waited till the Destroyers had taken their seats, then nodded to a grey-haired Wing Commander with World War One ribbons, who was one of the organization's executives. 'All right, Wing Commander, if you are ready for the briefing, I think my chaps are.'

The RAF officer got to his feet and limped to the centre of the room. 'Just call me Wingco,' he said expansively, running his eyes along the ranks of the Destroyers, who had returned from the Ringway Jump School that morning. 'All right, you've come to the end of training and I must say that you chaps have been the best course we've ever had. Top scores in everything!'

All the men were now dressed in Royal Air Force uniforms, including Crooke, promoted to the rank of squadron leader for the operation, their chests bearing the half wing of air gunners. That had been Mallory's idea, just in case the Hun interrogators started quizzing them about their technical knowhow. A knowledge of air gunnery was easier to fake than navigation or flight engineering. Mallory studied Crooke's new glass eye. Crooke had not liked the idea at first, but Mallory had insisted. 'What the devil would the Huns make of an air gunner who had only one eye?'

'Now one of our favourite camouflage containers is this.' The Wingco touched one of the gleaming brass buttons on his jacket. 'The top and bottom can be separated naturally and give a rather commodious space for hiding things. A couple of years back we unscrewed the button by turning it to the left – that is counter-clockwise. Naturally the boche soon found out that one. Nowadays they test all buttons on a suspected person's clothing by turning them that way. However,' he beamed broadly at them, as if he had just pulled a rabbit out of the hat to the tune of their applause, 'we are a bit smarter than the old Hun. We simply reversed the thread so that when they turned or twisted the button to the left it only served to tighten the assembly. Well, then we have another little trick which I might recommend to you.'

He pulled an ordinary khaki Army handkerchief out of his pocket. 'As you see a typical service snot rag, if you'll forgive the expression, gentlemen?' Again he beamed at them paternally, and held it up for them to see. 'But if we do this.' His thick fingers sought and found the key thread at the edge of the handkerchief. He pulled it. The brown disappeared to be replaced by a green colour, criss-crossed by a myriad lines. 'As you see now, we have a perfectly serviceable map of the Reich's western frontiers. Now what do you say to that, gentlemen?'

Stevens shifted momentarily on his seat and farted loudly.

'Excuse me, sir,' he said calmly. 'It just slipped out. Hope you don't mind – er – *Wingco?*'

The officer looked at him for a second, then, reassured by Stevens' apparent sincerity, he said hastily, 'No, no, it's those damned beans they served at lunch, no doubt. Well, let's get on with it. The mind of the boche is not too flexible. For that reason we decided to take an ordinary cigarette lighter and...'

As he fumbled in his pocket for the next piece of operational mumbo-jumbo, Mallory decided it was time to stop him.

'Wing Commander,' he interrupted. 'I'm really sorry to have to butt in to your fascinating exposé, but time's running out.' He made a play of looking at his expensive wrist watch, presented to him by one of his many titled if somewhat elderly female admirers.

'Is it?'

'I'm afraid so, and we're expected down at the US base at Chicksands for the evening briefing.'

The elderly RAF officer dropped his trick cigarette lighter back into his pocket. 'Then I'd better hush up, hadn't I?'

The hearty smile disappeared from his face as Mallory crossed to the door and opened it expectantly. 'Do you want me to go now?'

'I'd appreciate it, sir,' Mallory said smoothly, compromising on his old principle that one only called God and the Monarch sir.

Reluctantly the Wing Commander left. Mallory closed the door firmly behind him and turned to face his men. Stevens shook his head in wonder. 'Forgive my French, sir, but them SOE chaps don't know their arses from their elbows,' he said in his normal cockney accent, relinquishing his fruity 'Colonel Stevens' voice that he had acquired when he had run the black market operation in the desert during the period of his desertion. 'What a lot of old cobblers – him and his sodding magic buttons!'

'Yah,' Lone Star Alamo Jones drawled contemptuously, 'a real crock of shit.'

Peters looked at both of them threateningly. He had never lost his traditional respect for officers. Thaelmann and Gippo were pre-occupied with their own thoughts, though the half breed's fingers were toying absently with the small bag of gold coins which the SOE gave to all its agents.

'All right then, this is the drill,' Mallory said. 'About a month ago, one hundred RAF officers who escaped from a POW camp in Poland disappeared. We have reason to think that they have been murdered, probably by the Gestapo.'

Swiftly he sketched in the Prime Minister's fears, emphasizing his points with jabs of his fountain pen, while they listened in silence. There was a long pause after he finished until Crooke finally broke the silence. 'All right, Commander, and what is to be our role? It's obvious that we haven't gone through para training and all the rest of it these last two weeks for nothing?'

Mallory nodded. 'Yes,' he said drily.

'Naturally not...' He hesitated. Two weeks before when he and Godfrey had worked out the details of the operation it had seemed strange enough; now it appeared absolutely crazy. He took the plunge. 'I want you and your men to fly into Germany – and then be taken prisoner by the Germans!'

'*Crikey!*' Stevens breathed in awe and amazement. 'That's a ruddy turn-up for the books.'

He hurried on. 'You will take part in a normal bombing raid and a hit will be faked on your bomber, necessitating an emergency drop on your part – hence the para training. Once you have been taken prisoner, you'll escape. Again the reason for the "Wingco", his briefing and all the rest of the SOE training.' He paused and looked at them, noting the expression of complete disbelief growing on their faces; he could understand it well enough.

'Kiss me muvver, for I'm to be the Queen of the May.' Stevens, as always, was the first to react, but there was no humour in his eyes.

'And what are we gonna do for our third act, Commander,' the American sneered, 'crawl up our own asses and disappear?'

Mallory felt his annoyance overcome his

doubts. He did not like Jones; the man always rubbed him up the wrong way. He pointed his fountain pen at the Texan, a cold-blooded killer who had served in at least four different armies. 'Yes, just that, Jones,' he snapped. 'You'll disappear again – behind the bars of the special cage the Jerries run for people who look as if they are going to be troublemakers, as will un-doubtedly be the case with you.'

'Ya can betcha bottom dollar on that one, Commander,' Yank drawled, in no way put out by the sharpness of Mallory's answer. 'I hate Krauts.'

'All Germans are not Nazis, Yank,' Thaelmann said quietly but firmly. 'There are many–'

'Be quiet!' Crooke sharply restored order and turned back to face Mallory. 'And then, Commander, what is our mission?'

'You are to find the person who runs that camp, for it's our guess that it was that individual who killed our men. And you've got to kill him in such a spectacular manner that not one of his associates, however fanatical, will ever dare to kill another British POW.'

'I see,' Crooke said thoughtfully. 'But who is this person we are to kill?'

'That's the problem – we don't know. If I may recap, we have three bits of knowledge in our possession. The survivor, the one I told you about, was picked up in the *Dreilaendereck*, which roughly translates as "three countries corner". Am I right, Thaelmann?'

'Yes, sir. It's that area below Aachen, covering Holland, Belgium and Germany. It's rough country. Before the war it used to be a smugglers' paradise. All the people there speak the same German dialect and are intermarried across the three borders. They're a close community. They stick together against the authorities. They are an example of international working-class solidarity.'

Mallory groaned softly. 'No sermons please, Thaelmann. Well because of the people and the nature of the countryside, our Air Intelligence people tell shot-down RAF aircrew to make for it and hope that the Dutch underground can pick them up. So we might guess that the special camp where they tortured the poor fellow was in the Rhineland somewhere.' He tapped his finger with the fountain pen. 'That's point one. Point two, the man had been terribly tortured. They'd even emasculated him.'

'What in hell's name does that mean?'

'That they cut his balls off!'

'Jesus!'

'But before the Gestapo can torture anyone, the official concerned has to get permission from Himmler himself. My guess, therefore, is that the person we're looking for is a big wheel. I don't think Himmler would give any twopenny-half-penny counter-jumper permission to do the sort of thing I saw in that hospital.' He let them absorb the information, then he produced the bottle. 'When the Dutch Resistance chaps found him, he was holding this in his hand and he clung on to it like grim death.' He passed it to them. Slowly it moved from hand to hand.

Thaelmann studied it for a moment. 'Made in Cologne,' he commented.

'Yes. Perhaps another clue to the Rhineland. But at all events, it must have meant a lot to him. He was still hanging on to it when he died.'

'Not much to go on, sir,' Stevens said.

Mallory nodded, realizing once again just how impossible the mission was. 'I know. But I'm relying on you all. You're the best we've got. The PM asked for you personally to conduct the op.'

Crooke, a fanatical admirer of the great Prime Minister who in the previous November had told a Mansion House audience that he had not become 'the King's First Minister in order to preside over the liquidation of the British Empire,' said firmly, 'You can rely on us, Commander. We shall do the best we can, rest assured.'

Again it was Stevens who brought them down to earth. 'All right, sir, let's say we get that far. We find the bloke who murdered our chaps. But what are we gonna do him in with? All that lark about buttons and handkerchiefs won't sodding help us much.'

It was a question that Mallory had been expecting for the past hour. He raised the little black fountain pen, which had been the only piece of SOE mumbo-jumbo that had appealed to him when he had checked it out two days before. 'This,' he said, pointing it very carefully at Peters' cap which lay on the windowsill behind him. His thumb hit the plunger. There was a hiss of compressed air and a tiny .22 inch slug shot through the air. A hole appeared in the cap and the badge flew off and rattled to the floor.

5

In the briefing room, the Intelligence Officer of the USAAF bombing group with which they would fly at dawn pulled away a screen from the map running the length of the top wall of the Nissen hut. Two hundred sleepy Eighth Air Force men leaned forward to see the target for the day. An officer in a leather flying helmet whistled softly.

A red string, illuminated by the spotlights in the roof, stretched from the south of England to a pinpoint deep in Germany and then continued through the Brenner Pass over Italy and on to some desert airfield in North Africa.

The Intelligence Officer tapped the map with his pointer. 'Your primary today,' he said, 'is Regensburg.'

There was a low murmur from the men. Someone said, 'Jesus H. Christ! Not that again.'

The Intelligence Officer ignored the comment. 'Your aiming point is the centre of the Messerschmitt 109 engine assembly shops.

As far as this bombardment group is concerned, this is the most vital target we've ever gone after. If you guys knock it out, you've put paid to thirty per cent of the Luftwaffe's single-engined fighter production. And I guess I don't have to tell you fellers what that means to you personally. We'll go in in two boxes, consisting of a combat wing each, crossing the Dutch coast at zero plus ten and zero plus twenty. I don't have to tell you that the gaps in the timing are necessary because all the guys going to Regensburg will be carrying Tokio tanks. Naturally they'll have slower i.a.s than the other...'

The Intelligence Officer droned on, while the air crews scribbled down the instructions. Crooke nudged Mallory. 'We've made our appearance, Commander. Can we get out now? These Americans heat their places too much for me.'

Mallory nodded.

'Major Hartmann,' he said softly to the American next to him, 'do you think that your co-pilot could manage the details by himself? It's too hot in here and I'd like you to brief my own people.'

The American pilot looked like an 18-year-old schoolboy with his cap stuck on the back of his carefully combed hair, but Mallory knew he was at least thirty. 'Sure, Commander.' He threw a quick glance at his co-pilot. 'I guess Charley's a big boy now. He can take care of it himself. What do you say, Charley?'

Charley, a bald-headed second lieutenant, who looked all of forty, glanced up from his pad. 'Sure, Major, I can cope.'

Making as little noise as possible, but satisfied that they had been seen by the Air Force men, the little group followed Hartmann into the next room, guarded, as was the briefing room, by an armed 'snowdrop', a hard-faced American military policeman. 'All right, fellers,' Hartmann said when they had all sat down, 'I'll make it short and I hope sweet.'

Somewhere a gramophone was playing 'Honky Tonk Train Blues' and there was the smell and sizzle of eggs and bacon. The cooks were already busy, getting the aircrews' breakfast ready.

'Let me say that this is the craziest mission I've ever flown – okay, okay, Commander,' he added hurriedly. 'I'm not asking any questions, don't worry! All right, this is the deal. We'll carry out the Regensburg mission, going in with the first box so as not to get too much flak. I hope.' He crossed his fingers swiftly, a grin on his youthful features.

Stevens nudged Peters, 'He's a nice lad, ain't he?'

Peters agreed.

'Once we leave the target – let's say twenty miles south of Regensburg,' the Major continued, 'I'll simulate an emergency. Charley, the co-pilot, well he...'

'Charley knows nothing of your mission,' Mallory interrupted sharply. 'Nor is he to, or anyone else in the crew for that matter. Do you all understand?'

They muttered something unintelligible and Hartmann went on. 'Well Charley usually hands the controls over to me when we've cleared the target, so he'll not suspect anything. Okay, so I'll simulate an emergency and tell everybody to stand by for baling out. You guys will go then. As soon as you're out, I'll pretend to clear the emergency and as far as the rest of the crew is concerned, you've just had a bit of bad luck.' He shrugged. 'Tough shit, eh?'

He glanced at his watch. 'Okay fellers, that's about it, as far as I'm concerned. You can get yourselves some chow next door. I just want to check out my crew. This is my last mission and I don't want to screw it up.'

Crooke waited till he had gone, then he turned to the others. 'All right, go and get yourselves something to eat.' They all filed out, leaving Crooke alone with Mallory. At once Crooke moved over and whispered something in the Commander's ear.

Mallory looked at him aghast. 'You can't mean that?' he said hollowly.

'I do. It's the only way.'

'But he's such a nice chap. We can't do that, honestly!'

Crooke ignored his protests. 'If you won't call C to request permission, I will,' he said firmly. 'Nothing can be allowed to jeopardize this mission.' For a full five minutes they argued. In the end Mallory gave in and called the head of Secret Intelligence.

He was not too happy to be woken up at White's, but he jumped at Crooke's proposal with alacrity. 'Yes,' he said, 'I'll clear it with the PM. Kill them all – it's the only way to preserve our security.'

At 7.30 the B-17 broke out of the cloud into the glare of the rising sun, a blood-red ball on the horizon. Below the English countryside was still blanketed in thick mist. Slowly the great four-engined bomber continued to rise, burdened as it was with its bomb-load and the wing-tip Tokio tanks, which would keep it flying eleven hours.

One by one the Destroyers went up to the co-pilot's seat, where by staring over Charley's shoulder, they could see the great armada stretched out as far as the eye could penetrate through the thin air. Here and there pilots were still firing their red, green and yellow flares as they tried to identify themselves and fit into their respective flights. But slowly the three squadrons flying in the first box for Regensburg were falling into line behind their fiery commander, Colonel Curtis Le May, a stickler for a tight formation.

Hartmann let each of them have his turn, then he walked back to where they were crouched in the fuselage next to the gunners in the side blisters. 'All right, fellers,' he said, 'we're going on oxygen in a minute, so I'll be grateful to you if you stay put. If anyone wants to use the can at the back.' He indicated the drum which acted as a latrine in the darkness at the rear, 'take the little bottle of juice with you. In about five minutes the gunners will test their fifty-calibres.' He nodded to the gunners crouched five feet away, their fur caps pulled well down over their heads. 'No sweat. It's just practice.' The grin vanished momentarily from his face. 'The real shooting'll start as soon as we hit the Dutch coast. OK?' They nodded their understanding and clipped on the oxygen masks. The flight continued.

Two hours later they crossed the coast of Holland. The first flak blossomed up around them. Shards of hot metal rapped at their egg-shell of perspex and aluminium like the beak of some gigantic bird. The Destroyers looked at each other over their clumsy oxygen masks and Crooke knew what must have been going on in their minds at that moment. They were over Occupied Europe; there was no turning back now.

At 10.40, as they were crossing the Belgian-German border near Eupen, the trouble started. 'Fighters at two o'clock – low!' one of the gunners' voices crackled through the intercom to which the Destroyers were also hooked in. Their heads swung to the front of the plane. Over Hartmann's shoulder they could see two Focke-Wulf 190s turning and whizzing through the bombers ahead. They were making a bold frontal attack, flashing in at a 600 mph rate of closure, their cannon

65

chattering. The Destroyers ducked instinctively. The German fighters broke off at the very last moment. But their attack had paid off.

Three hundred yards ahead of them a Fort blew up in a great slow balloon of fire. Desperately Hartmann fought the turbulence. Crooke stole a quick look at his men. Sweat had broken out in great beads on their foreheads in spite of the icy cold of the fuselage. They were scared, he knew. More so because they were so helpless. A few minutes later the Germans started to hit the great box of bombers with everything they had. The radio started to crackle with the urgent messages from their own crew and those of other ships. 'Yellow noses twelve o'clock high... Look out skipper! Two of the bastards coming in from port ... four more two o'clock low!...'

Hartmann was a veteran. They could hear him keeping the crew under control, as the rear gunner and the one positioned directly above the cockpit went into action against the German fighters zooming in from all sides: 'Don't throw rounds away, Joe... Pilot to rear gunner, don't yell like that... Talk slow... Lead 'em more... Pilot to top gunner, short bursts ... for Chrissake, short bursts...'

The Fort droned on. In front of them another plane was hit. A silver rectangle of metal sailed past the cockpit – a B-17's main exit door. An instant later it was followed by a small dark object. It hurtled through the box, barely missing several props. It was a man, making a delayed drop, his body crouched up, revolving like a crack diver attempting a triple somersault. Hardly had he disappeared from sight, when the B-17 blew up in a violent ball of flame and smoke. When it had cleared, all that was visible were four balls of fire, the fuel tanks, streaming downwards.

The Fort rocked violently. The fuselage was filled with smoke. There was an acrid, bitter smell and the floor of the bomber was suddenly littered with shining aluminium debris. Among it lay one of the two waist gunners, his body stretched out in the extravagant posture of the violently done to death. Crooke unclipped his mask attachment. He grabbed one of the portable oxygen bottles and, clipping it on, hurried to the shambles at the back of the plane, swaying from side to side as Hartmann took violent evasive action.

The lights had fused in the rear and the smoke made it difficult to see what had happened. A figure loomed up. The rear gunner was bare-headed and without an oxygen mask. 'I've been hit,' he gasped and staggering forward, collapsed into Crooke's arm. Gently Crooke lowered him to the deck. He was dead before he reached it.

Crooke flung a quick glance behind him. The Yank had taken over the fifty-calibre machine-gun in the waist, standing astride the dead gunner. Behind him Peters was manning the port gun where the other sergeant gunner was clutching his shattered knee. Both were intent on the attacking fighters. No one was paying any attention to him. In the next five seconds he had taken some sticky, puttylike substance from inside his jacket, thrust a detonator into its centre, lifted the dead gunner, shored the explosive under him and lowered the body again. He had just passed sentence of death on the unsuspecting crew of the Fort.

Desperately Hartmann fought to keep in his box. Twice in the past ten minutes his wingmen had been shot out of the sky and Le May's voice had come crackling over the radio, 'Hartmann – for Chrissake, *close up!*' Now the Kraut fighters were literally queuing up waiting to let the Forts have it.

The air was full of flying debris from both the Forts and their attackers – exit doors, emergency hatches, prematurely open parachutes, great shining sheets of aluminium – and bodies.

The minutes dragged past and still the fighters came in. Hartmann felt his control begin to go. His body was drenched in sweat. He tried to tell himself it was happening to someone else. On past missions he had been able to do that and watch the slaughter as if it were an animated cartoon in a movie theatre. But not on this one. He realized he had used his stock of courage. He was a burned-out case. Thank God this was his last mission!

Above them the top-gunner's twin muzzles burst into life again, only a foot above his head. He jumped in his seat. 'Charley,' he said, his voice cracked and unnatural, 'you take over now.'

The old man looked at him over the edge of his mask. Ahead the fiery parasite upon the body of the stricken city started to writhe into life as the incendiaries began to do their work. Charley nodded and Hartmann sank back into the seat. Let Charley look after it now.

The glow from the ground filled the

cockpit with its sinister light. The plane began to rock. Every now and again the Fort shook like a small ship hitting a solid wall of water. Hartmann felt the tension rise in his stomach. He braced himself in his seat, feeling his buttocks contract. Behind him the waist gunners still hammered away.

The bombardier's voice crackled over the intercom. 'On target.' Hartmann, crouched in the protection of his seat, did not raise himself to look at the great Me-109 workshops lying below in the curve of the Danube, just outside Regensburg. The flak burst around them once again. The plane rocked from side to side as if pushed by some gigantic hand. Hartmann tried to control himself. He felt himself clutching the sides of his seat with hands that dripped with sweat. Suddenly he found himself praying, screaming a plea to heaven for rescue, a way out of this burning hell.

'An S-turn to starboard, Skipper,' the bombardier, intent on his target, ordered.

'Enough!' he cried. 'On heading now.'

The plane droned on. Hartmann shut his eyes. The bombardier's calm New England voice cut into his consciousness. 'Steady, Skipper ... steady ... Great, Skipper, we're on target.'

Suddenly the B-17 gave a slight lift. Hartmann opened his eyes. The red light on the instrument panel had gone out.

'Bombs gone!' the bombardier's voice cried joyfully.

Hartmann craned forward to look out of the perspex. A great pillar of black smoke was rising from the Me-109 plant.

We got the bastard!' Charley yelled.

Hartmann licked his cracked lips. 'Yeah,' he said, trying to control his voice, as Charley swung the plane round and the snow-capped Alps began to loom up in the distance.

Hastily Hartmann pulled himself together. It was nearly over and he hadn't cracked after all. He pulled off his gauntlets and wiped the sweat off his palms. 'Okay, Charley,' he said in his normal voice, 'I'll take the old bitch now.'

He could hear Charley breathe a sigh of relief over the intercom.

'Thanks, Skipper. I'd appreciate that. Those last ten minutes knocked the piss out of me.'

Hartmann took over the controls. His old professionalism reasserted itself. Expertly his eyes flicked over the myriad dials. In spite of the hit, they were all functioning correctly. He raised the revs, a little pleased with himself. 'Not bad for a sixty-day wonder,' he told himself. 'Get me the Air Medal at least.'

Ten minutes later he faked the emergency. 'Charley,' he said urgently. 'Hold your water, but number one engine's aborting.'

'Jesus,' Charley breathed.

'No sweat,' he lied, pleased with himself now. 'I think I can hold the bitch. But get to the rear and tell those RAF Joes to stand by with their chutes. We might have to bale out.'

'Wilco, Skipper.' Hastily Charley seized his bottle and went to where the Destroyers squatted, pale-faced and sick-looking, in the debris-littered shambles of the fuselage.

'Stand by with your parachutes,' he ordered. 'No need for panic, but you guys might have to bale out. We got an emergency.'

A frenzy of gloved-hand fumbling and they had fixed their chutes. Hastily they followed Charley, slipping and stumbling over the debris, to where they would jump.

Up front, Hartmann feathered number one prop. The big bomber gave a series of violent lurches. Charley's eyes above his mask grew round with fear. He knew what

72

the noise meant.

Hartmann's voice crackled over the intercom. 'Skipper here. Charley, get 'em ready to go. The sonuvabitch is dying on me. Tell the crew to stand by. Only the limeys go – first!'

'OK, Skipper.'

He pushed by the Destroyers. With a shove he released the main exit. He pulled back just in time as it flew off into space. Freezing air rushed in. The fuselage was flooded with the roar and stutter of the Fort's engines.

'Okay,' Charley shouted through the intercom, 'out you go, one by one – and, for Chrissake, remember not to pull the ripcord till you're clear of the plane! Or the props'll give you one helluva short haircut.'

He patted Gippo on the back. 'You!'

The half-breed, his face a strange greenish hue, hesitated, as he stared at the ground below.

The Yank acted swiftly. He raised his boot and planted a hearty kick in Gippo's backside. He flew out of the door. One by one they followed him until it was Crooke's turn. He cast a quick look behind him to where Hartmann was hunched over the controls. Charley thought he was scared and

73

tapped him on the shoulder. Angrily Crooke pushed away his hand and launched himself into space.

His breath was dragged from his lungs. Then the parachute opened and his arms were jerked almost from their sockets, as the canopy opened. As he swung from side to side, he caught glimpses of the countryside below – patches of dark firs in the valley with the snow-covered hills to their right.

Reaching up, as he had been taught at the parachute school at Ringway, he caught the shroud lines and pulled on them. The pendulum motion ceased. He was coming down in a relatively straight line.

Crooke craned his neck so that he could see the sky above him. It was dotted with the dark shapes of the Forts. Here and there, smoke poured from a stricken plane limping after the rest. Nearly twenty minutes had gone by since he had hidden the P.E. under the dead gunner's body. It should happen any moment if it were going to happen at all. Anxiously, he scanned the sky. The planes continued to drone on towards Italy and safety. In a few hours' time they would be touching down on some North African landing strip in brilliant sunshine. There'd be the usual kissing of the ground, followed by a noisy breakfast of bacon and eggs – with whisky for those who needed it. De-briefing and it would be all over – till the next time. Then it happened. A Fort in the middle of the last group of stragglers suddenly erupted into flame. A sheet of yellow fire shot along its belly. The tail unit broke off and began to sail downwards like some huge black leaf, twirling round and round as it fell. The Fort's nose dropped. Without its tail no pilot in the world could save the stricken plane. Smoke and flame streaming from it, it plummeted to the earth at 400 mph.

It had all happened too fast for the crew to have had time to bale out. Moments later it crashed into one of the snow-covered hills in the distance.

Crooke clapped his legs together as he had been taught. The branches of the firs tore at his clothes, but they also broke his fall. He hardly felt the impact as he hit the frozen ground. All the same he was winded. For a moment he lay there, swamped in the chute, fighting for breath. There was no sound now, save the soft rustle of the firs in the wind and the dying drone of the bombers. Finally he rose. Taking his time, he began to free himself from the parachute harness.

Now he could hear the baying of the dogs and the angry shouts of the searchers getting closer. Leisurely he folded up his chute. He tapped the pocket of his flying jacket, to check if the fountain pen were there. It was.

'*Hier ... zu mir, Leute... Ich habe ihn doch gesehen.*' The hoarse cries grew louder. He could hear their booted feet crashing through the undergrowth. A red-faced policeman in a green ankle-length overcoat burst through the trees. In his hand he held a big pistol. It was shaking and there was fear in his eyes. '*Haende hoch, oder ich schiesse!*' he yelled at the top of his voice, the Luger shaking violently.

Calmly Crooke let the chute drop and raised his arms.

Something whacked him hard behind the ear. Everything went black and he sank to his knees.

SECTION TWO: THE KRIEGIES

'I don't want to dishearten you, gentlemen, but we've never had a successful escape from Stalag Luft VIIb'

*Grey, Stalag Luft VIIb Escape
Officer, to the Destroyers.*

1

'Well, gentlemen,' said the interrogating officer, a plump captain in the *Luftwaffe* with a round schoolmaster's face, 'I have myself lived in England – at Oxford.' He beamed proudly at the name. 'I am knowing your country well. You and I will be friends, yes?'

Of the six bedraggled prisoners lined up in front of him, only Stevens deigned to answer. Even in captivity he was irrepressible. 'When was that, sir?' he asked with feigned interest.

Hauptmann Koske beamed. 'Well,' he began, winding up slowly like most schoolmasters who had learned that the day was long and they had to string out their little bits of knowledge from nine to four. 'It must have been in 1932, yes – just before the Fuhrer was coming to power...'

'Do you know the Fuhrer personally?' Stevens interrupted, adding a hasty *'sir'*.

Crooke flashed him a sharp look. The SOE instructor had told them the less they said the better.

'No, I have not yet had that honour,' the Hauptmann said. Then he caught the look in Stevens' eye and wagged his fat finger at him in mock warning. 'Ah, you are pulling my arm, as the English say, no?'

Stevens looked shocked. 'No, sir, I wouldn't dare do anything like that. I just wanted to know whether you had ever seen the Fuhrer. You see, sir, I'd like to know something about him.'

'And what is that?' The Hauptmann fell for Stevens' pitch hook, line and sinker.

'Well, sir,' Stevens pretended difficulty in the formulation of his query. 'I want to know whether you knew whether the Fuhrer wore...' He broke off abruptly.

The Hauptmann was intrigued. 'Go on,' he prompted, 'go on.'

Stevens licked his lips. 'Well, sir, it's just that I'd like to know whether the Fuhrer wears ladies' knickers!'

Behind them the elderly NCO in charge of the guard guffawed out loud. Obviously he understood English.

The little Hauptmann flushed crimson. '*Schnauze!*' he bellowed at the laughing NCO.

The man's laughter froze on his face. He stared woodenly at some point behind the seated officer's shoulder.

'Now, now.' The interrogator caught himself in time. 'We must not be making jokes like that, must we?'

Stevens said nothing. But he winked solemnly at the others.

Thus the interrogation started.

It was what they had expected. 'We call it the sweet-sour approach,' their SOE instructor had explained, 'like Chink food. Your interrogator will first play Herr Nasty. Bang-bang and you'll go to the concentration camp, if you don't spill the beans. Then he'll be Herr Nice. What a bloody awful war this is, but we fighting men must stick together regardless of our nationalities and all that sort of cock. He'll become a charming friend. Like a fag and a cup of coffee? The usual soft soap. When the coffee arrives he'll keep it till you're gasping for a drink. Finally he hands it over and just when you're going to lift it to your grateful lips, he bangs it out of your hand and sends it flying.'

The Hauptmann, who was obviously working hard at his job in the *Heimat* to avoid the death sentence of the Russian front, used both tacks. One by one he had them in his little office and tried the same routine on all of them. 'Of course,' he told

81

them, 'as far as the Royal Air Force is concerned you have been killed during the raid. No one has registered you with the Red Cross. Naturally then we are being able to send you to a certain place if you are not co-operating.' In spite of the fractured English, the threat was obvious: speak up or it's the concentration camp.

Predictably he went from there to the typical approach of that year when after El Alamein and Stalingrad it was clear that Germany was losing the war. 'Now, we are all friends together, are we not? I am not wanting to make life hard for you.' Out would come the cigarettes looted from the prisoners' Red Cross parcels which were never delivered. 'Let us smoke one together.' A fake smile would play around his fat, well-fed cheeks. 'After all we are from the same race and should concern ourselves more with the fight against the Red hordes in the East than with each other. Germany and England should be friends.'

Afterwards that same evening Stevens commented dourly to Gippo sitting opposite him in the damp, yellow-lit cell, gnawing on a crust of hard black German Army bread. 'And I suppose he was going to have you turned into soap in the concentration camps, you black bastard?'

'No,' Gippo answered without offence. 'Me, I am going to be made into an honorary Aryan!'

But in spite of the Luftwaffe Hauptmann's stupidity, Crooke was taking no chances of being caught out at this early stage of the mission. The Destroyers' backgrounds were too varied and easily probed. Besides not one of them knew enough of aircrew work to be able to stand up to skilled cross-examination. As he knew from the SOE instructor, the best way to avoid suspicion was to let the interrogator know a little and make it appear that he had discovered the information off his own bat.

When he came up for his second grilling, he carefully dropped the necessary titbits of information without making it too obvious that he was giving them away.

By continual movement of his right eye, he drew the fat sweating *Luftwaffe* captain's attention to the left one, made of glass, and watched with satisfaction as the ex-schoolmaster scribbled something on his pad. He could well imagine what it would be: active member of RAF aircrew, yet has serious physical disability. Half an hour later the German asked him the same old question, which he had put to them all time and time again in the past forty-eight hours. 'Now, Squadron Leader, why is it that six members of the Royal Air Force were flying with the Americans?'

Crooke pretended to lose his temper. 'Because our authorities are bloody-well sick of missing the target at...' He appeared to catch himself in time. 'I have nothing to say,' he said coldly.

The Hauptmann could hardly repress his smile. Crooke could well imagine the thought running through his schoolmaster's brain. 'The RAF is sick of the errors inherent in night-time bombing. They were considering daylight attacks. Hence the presence of the RAF men on this 8th USAAF raid.

Thereafter his cross-examination was desultory. He beamed at Crooke as the latter rose to go and pressed a handful of cigarettes on him. 'For the chaps,' he whispered confidentially. 'The guard will not say anything.'

As Crooke closed the door and marched down the stone corridor, escorted to his cell by the elderly NCO who had laughed at Stevens' joke on the first day, the Hauptmann could hardly wait to begin his report to higher headquarters. 'Recent interrogation of six RAF officer POWs indicates that the Royal Air Force might be going over to daylight raiding. All of the POWs were mature men and looked experienced aircrew members (their senior officer was minus one eye and a pilot officer seconded from the Indian Air Force was wearing many medal ribbons indicating pre-war service experience). In addition, all were air gunners which doubtless means that the RAF is considering the problem of heavier armament which would be necessary for daylight terror raids…'

As he planned the report in his head, he told himself that it would keep him from the Russian front for another six months at least. There might even be a spot of leave in it for him.

One day later the Destroyers were moved to Stalag Luft VIIb. Their period of interrogation was finished. They were over the first hurdle.

The ancient wood-burning truck bumped up the rutted track to Stalag Luft VIIb, typical of the hundreds of POW camps which dotted Germany in the February of 1943. Several acres of hard-packed earth, which turned to thick mud when the rains came in the spring, shaped in the form of a hexagon by the high triple wire fences. These fifteen-foot electrified fences were presided over by stork-legged watchtowers, containing elderly reservists and mutilated veterans of the Russian front, armed with Spandau machine guns. Fierce Alsatian dogs patrolled between the fences ready at a signal from their handlers to go for a man's throat – or his testicles.

Inside the compound were four neat lines of dark wooden huts, built on piles so that the 'goons', as Crooke already knew from the SOE instructor, the German guards were called, could probe under them with their long metal rods for contraband and attempts to start a tunnel.

Thaelmann, who had escaped from Dachau ten years before, ran his eyes anxiously over the place. Pale-faced prisoners were gathering in the courtyard to welcome the new arrivals. The gate swung slowly open and several scruffy grey-uniformed guards came out of their hut to take charge. Peters turned to Crooke and said morosely, 'Well, sir, you got us out of one camp six months ago easily enough.' He was referring to the military prison in Egypt from which Crooke had recruited them. 'I

86

hope you can get us out of this bugger as easily.'

As soon as the truck stopped, the POWs swarmed around them, shouting excited questions. They were dressed in a motley of clothing, ranging from complete RAF officers' outfits to strange combinations of civvie rags and bits and pieces of uniform. A number of them wore huge wooden clogs in place of shoes. But in spite of their clothing and their pinched, undernourished faces, Crooke could see that they were in great heart; they had not lost their fighting spirit.

'*Meine Herren!*' A middle-aged sergeant with one sleeve empty and a black wound medal prominent on his chest, forced his way through the crowd, followed by the guard. 'You must please remove yourselves,' he ordered.

'Go on,' a score of voices shouted. 'Give us a chance, Fritz! We want to talk to the new boys!'

But the sergeant forced his way to the new arrivals and pushed back the crowd patiently and with good-humour. The guards fell in around them, their rifles pointing at the crowd. The POWs moved back reluctantly and made way for the Destroyers who were marched off to the administration building with a black and white sign saying KOM-MANDANTUR over the door. They passed inside. 'All right, gentlemen,' the sergeant said, 'off with the clothes. First you wash.' He indicated the showers in the room to the right.

The Destroyers did not need a second invitation. They hadn't washed since they had been captured and Stevens, struggling to get off his uniform, commented joyfully, 'I'm beginning to pong like a gorilla's armpit!'

The sergeant finally drove them out of the showers by turning up the water until it was scalding hot. 'Now you will be searched,' he ordered, as they stood around naked.

Swiftly he and his men started to examine their discarded clothing. Their money was taken away. Their identity documents followed. Then one of the searchers came across a fountain pen. He held it up to the one-armed NCO. *'Herr Feldwebel, was machen wir hiermit?'*

'That's a souvenir, sergeant,' Peters said. 'We've all got one – RAF issue.' He made a gesture with his big hand, as if he were putting something behind his back surreptitiously. He had seen captured *Afrika Korps* men do it in the desert when they had tried to explain that they had stolen something. 'We organized them.'

The NCO's suspicious look relaxed. '*Schon gut,*' he snapped at the private, '*die können die Dinge behalten.*'

The NCO waited until his men were finished with the clothes. Then he beckoned the private who had found the first pen. Wordlessly the soldier ran the rubber finger stall on the NCO's forefinger. The NCO was obviously embarrassed.

'Gentlemen, I must now search you in your private organs. I do not like.' He shrugged. 'But it is orders. You understand?'

One by one they were ordered forward. Swiftly the private searched under their arms, ran his fingers through their hair and then indicated they should bend down for the anal search.

When it was Stevens' turn, he simpered. 'Oh, this is going to be a real thrill. Kiss me quick, yer mother's drunk. Hey, sarge, be careful! What yer trying to do? *Go all the way to the Khyber Pass!*'

As he raised himself he caught a glimpse of a pale-faced bespectacled German looking in through the window, his mouth open, as if he were finding it difficult to breathe. When he saw that Stevens had seen him, he disappeared. The NCO caught the direction of Stevens' gaze. A strange look crossed his face. 'That's the head of our section. Hauptmann Suess. You'd better watch him.'

Over the next hour, they were given a short haircut, had their photographs taken and were handed aluminium disks, bearing their new POW numbers.

The NCO wagged a thick forefinger at them paternally. 'Let me say to you, gentlemen, if you behave yourselves, you will have no trouble. You are now prisoners of war.'

'Aw, go and crap in ya hat!' the Yank snapped.

The NCO shrugged wearily. He had seen it all before. A couple of months in Stalag Luft VIIb would tame them; it always did.

Two hours later they were released into the body of the camp and after answering the excited questions of the members of the various hut messes to which they were assigned, they were summoned to meet the Senior British Officer, Wing Commander Smythe.

Smythe, a clipped-moustached, grey-haired officer with his collar neatly pressed by means of a can of hot water, was obviously a pre-war regular. Crooke could tell the type at once. Rules and regulations, that would be the tune he would play, Crooke told himself, even before the Wing Commander started his traditional lecture to new arrivals.

'Gentlemen, you will obviously try to escape. It is expected of you. However, I should like to point out to you that everything you can think of has been done before. When I first came here in forty, for instance, there was a Polish chap who tried to get out in the cart that cleans the latrines. He got in the ghastly thing naked, with his clothes tied up in a macintosh. The boche caught him of course. They always do. In forty-one there were two crazy Australians who tried to pole-vault the wire. And what did they get for their pains? One a badly torn up chest and the other a burst of machine gun bullets in the guts. Last year we did better. We got six out through a tunnel, but the boche had been tipped off, it seems. They were waiting for them at Trier station where they had agreed to rendezvous before crossing the frontier into France.'

Crooke did not try to conceal his contempt. 'Are you trying to tell us, sir, that we should not try to get out?'

'Not at all, Squadron Leader. It's your duty to try to escape. All I am trying to say is that our score is not very good.'

'Bloody hell!' Stevens muttered to the others. 'What the hell is this – a bloody game of cricket!'

The Senior Officer glared at Stevens. For a moment there was a stony silence which was broken by a knock at the door. 'Come in,' the Senior Officer cried.

The door swung open to reveal a skinny, yellow-faced officer in his early thirties, wearing the brass 'VR' insignia of the Volunteer Reserve of his lapels but without the wings of an aircrew member on his chest. 'Flight Lieutenant Grey,' Smythe introduced the new man. 'Our Escape Officer, bagged in the desert in forty-one. Ground job.'

Grey nodded to them coolly. 'Hallo, chaps.' He did not offer to shake hands. He turned to the Senior Officer again.

'I checked their beds, sir.'

'Anything to report?'

'Nothing suspicious, except I found this.' He held up one of the gold sovereigns, which Gippo had wangled out of the SOE HQ.

'That's mine!' Gippo said angrily.

'How did you get it – and more importantly, how did you smuggle it in through the goons?'

'It's my good luck piece, which I always take with me on a flight. Smuggle it in? Easy. I am putting it underneath my tongue.'

Apparently satisfied, Grey flipped it to him. Gippo caught it neatly and tucked the coin away in his pocket.

'You must understand, gentlemen,' Smythe explained, 'that we always have to be on the lookout for plants. The boche have been known to put their own people into POW camps to spy on us. We have to take our precautions. All right, I'll turn you over to Grey now.'

Grey cleared his throat and stepped into the centre of the room. Outside a group of prisoners had started a game of soccer which was rapidly disintegrating into Stalag Luft VIIb's version of the Eton Wall Game. 'All right, let me make it short, sharp and *not* too sweet. You're new boys, full of good food and energy. Not like us, I'm afraid. So you'll try to escape. But as the Wing Commander has probably just explained to you, the camp just like the human body has its entrances and exits – and they are strictly limited. So don't get cocky. Let me explain some of the difficulties. First the goons, as we call the guards, under Hauptmann Suess. Most of them speak English, and some of them can lip-read. So even at a distance, you could be under surveillance. What else? Well, there are seismographic devices buried below the ground to record any vibration made by would-be tunnellers. What about the wire then? At night every bit of it is lit, in spite of the black-out. The Jerry knows our people wouldn't bomb this place. Bright as day, as you'll see tonight.'

'What about the wire at daytime?' Peters asked.

'Since the Australians tried their pole vault, the Germans have a trip wire running right around the camp, thirty feet inside the fence. Anyone who steps over knows he can be shot by the guards on the towers. Even when we play soccer, we keep a white coat on the goalpost and if the ball goes over the trip wire the chap who goes to get it puts on the coat and can easily be seen by the guards.

'All right, so you don't tunnel and you don't attempt the wire, what is left?' He answered his own question. 'The gate. But as Wing Commander Smythe has undoubtedly already pointed out, the goons there are no dummies and about every trick under the sun has been tried to get through it in one form of disguise or other. I don't want to dishearten you, gentlemen, but we've never had a successful escape from Stalag Luft VIIb.'

'So what do we do?' the Yank broke the silence. 'Fly out of the goddam place?'

Grey looked at him suspiciously. 'You're American,' he said. 'Why are you in here?'

'Eagle Squadron. Came over in forty to fight the war for you limeys.'

As Grey absorbed the information, Crooke turned to the Wing Commander, ignoring the Escape Officer, to whom he had taken an instinctive dislike.

'Am I to take it, sir,' he said, 'that you are advising us *not* to escape? Is that what this briefing is about?'

The Wing Commander flushed, but before he could answer, Grey beat him to it. 'Don't get the Wing Commander or me wrong. All we are trying to tell you is that you should give yourselves a couple of months to get acclimatized to the place – get settled in. Take a few courses first. We've got some wonderful woodworking classes going at the moment. And there's the camp's amateur dramatic society...'

'Jesus wept!' the American interrupted him with a moan. 'What the hell is this place, a rest home for limeys, who don't want to fight the war!'

Grey ignored the remark. 'Now gentleman, please have a look round before you start blowing your tops. A week in here will, I think, show you that I'm not talking out of the back of my head.' He reached in the bag on the trestle table and pulled out a handful of tins. 'You'll probably be needing a few fags till your Red Cross parcels start to arrive. I've drawn these from our central reserve. There are fifty fags in each tin. Please take one each; you can replace them when you get your first parcels.'

Crooke looked at him contemptuously. He did not attempt to pick up one of the proffered tins. He turned and began to walk to the door. The rest of the Destroyers followed.

Wing Commander Smythe looked at them in bewilderment. 'But I say, Squadron Leader, you mustn't be offended!' he stuttered.

'Gentlemen,' Grey urged, 'please come back.'

Gippo, who was bringing up the rear,

threw a quick glance at the two camp officers. Both were concentrating their attention on the departing Crooke. Swiftly he grabbed three of the precious cans, the main currency of the camp, and thrust them into his blouse.

As he passed Grey, he said in his best imitation of a British officer, 'You know what you can do with your bloody fags!'

2

The Destroyers spent the next forty-eight hours scouring the camp individually, dodging the 'hearties' indulging in physical jerks, the 'loners' walking round and round the circuit of the camp, and 'the funnies', engaged in a myriad strange activities from playing the flute in the solitude of the stinking latrines to attempting to distil whisky from a mixture of potato peelings and dried currants. After each *Appell* they met to discuss the fruits of their reconnaissances.

But as Crooke told them on the evening of the second day: 'Let's not be too hasty. Grey and that old fool of a Senior Officer might be war-weary, but they've been in here long enough to know the ropes. Let's give it another night before we make any decisions. Tomorrow midday when they're all feeding their faces we'll fight it out in the big latrine. See what we come up with.'

That night the Destroyers stayed awake to check the wire and the precautions the enemy took to guard it. When the arc-lights were turned on, they attempted to judge the depths and the position of the shadows. In the silence of the huts, broken only by the snores of their fellow *Kriegies,* they crouched at the windows, timing the sentries on their beats and trying to ascertain whether they changed their habits towards early morning when they would presumably be tired after a long night's guard. The following day, each having collected a piece of official brown lavatory paper, they made their way through the rain to the latrine.

Crooke had picked an ideal time and place for their conference. It was midday and the *Mittagessen,* boiled potatoes and salt fish, was the high point of the camp inmates' life – and it was raining hard.

Crooke waited till they were ready. 'All right,' he began, 'let's have what you found out.' He looked at Stevens. 'You can start.'

'There's a tunnel going. I spotted it in the first hour. All yesterday morning there was a stream of them coming out of hut five with the bags for carrying earth under their pants. They're dumping it in here. But not a hope for us. There's a waiting list. And the way they're going at it to try to get under them seismo … well, whatever yer call them – they'll still be digging in nineteen forty-five.'

'Jones?'

The Texan shook his head. 'The wire's negative. I checked around for tools. They've got some, but they're not giving any to the new boys; besides, those goddam hounds; if they ever got their teeth into you, you'd be a singing tenor in no time short.'

Crooke nodded to the guardsman. 'And you, Peters, did you have any better luck?'

'The gate's pretty tough, sir. The sentries are alert and soldierly, in spite of their age. Conscientious too. Yesterday they asked Captain Suess for his ID card as he came in from the camp here.' He shook his head slowly. 'There might be something we could do with his office. It's in the little wooden shack between the inner and outer ring of wire, but how we'd get through the first fence to it, I wouldn't know.'

Crooke made a mental note of the guardsman's point. He, too, had thought of the little hut between the two fences. It might be a way of overcoming the major obstacle, but how exactly he did not know. Through the open door of the latrine, which looked out on to the compound, he could see that the rain had changed to thick wet flakes of snow. 'What about Gippo? Anything?'

Gippo wagged a skinny finger to indicate

nothing. 'But one thing, sir. That escaping officer gentleman...?'

'You mean Grey?'

'Yes, that gentleman. Well, he is watching us. He has been looking you up all day yesterday – the lot of you.'

'Why?' Thaelmann asked suspiciously. Ever since they had been in the camp, his silence had deepened and his jerky movements indicated how nervous he was. The others knew why. In the desert he had sworn that he would never be taken prisoner again. Suicide was preferable to the agony of another Dachau. 'How do you know? What makes you think that?'

Gippo held up his hand. 'More than this I am not able to be telling you, but he was watching you – and last night in my mess, he's in my hut, he asked me something in Hindustani. Fortunately I have enough of the language to answer him to his satisfaction.' Crooke remembered with gratitude the half-breed's talent for languages, gained in Port Said before the war.

'And you, Thaelmann, what do you know?'

'I think I know something. I don't exactly know if we can use the information. It's Hauptmann Suess – he's what we call in

German *ein warmer Bruder.*'

'A warm brother?' Crooke translated. 'What the devil's that?'

Thaelmann's brow creased as he sought for the right word in English. 'A ... pederast?'

Five minutes later they were in the recreation hut, already thick with the smoke of after-lunch cigarettes and the pungent smell of boiled white cabbage which had been the main ingredient of the midday meal which the members of the amateur dramatic society had eaten, prior to the rehearsal of the 'Naughty Nineties'.

Already the improvised stage, which served as the chapel on Sundays, was graced by a dozen or so *Kriegies,* over-rouged and a little absurd in their short tight skirts and black stockings, who were adjusting their wigs and forming up into a crude chorus line.

'There he is,' Thaelmann whispered, as they filed into the benches at the back of the room. 'Over near the front.'

The German Captain was seated in the front row, a benign smile on his pale, moon-like face, as he gazed up at the 'dancers', now bathed in dusky red in the stagelights which had just been switched on. But his eyes were not fixed on the absurd chorus line with its shaven legs and plucked eyebrows: they were directed at a tall blond young man, whose decidedly female appearance in the long silver lamé gown he was wearing was marred somewhat by the big RAF flying boots on his feet and the pipe stuck between his teeth.

Stevens whistled softly. 'Oh la la, isn't he lovely... Give me another week in here without a bit of the other and I'll be thinking he's better than Betty Grable.'

'Shut up, Stevens,' Crooke snapped, 'and keep your voice down! For your information that's Flight Lieutenant Kean, twenty kills to his record and a double DFC. If he's a pansy, then you are too.'

Before Stevens could retort, a tall officer with an enormous red moustache, who was obviously the director, strode from somewhere off stage and began to wind up the gramophone. 'All right,' he bellowed, 'pull yer knickers up, girls, and get in line.' Then men shuffled into their places. 'Kean.' The man with the pipe put down his lines on the piano. 'Get your wig on and hide these bloody boots.'

'Roger,' the beautiful young man answered

dutifully. He placed his pipe next to the lines and adjusted a long blond wig over his own hair.

Crooke's eyes were reserved for the German officer staring at the young fighter pilot. The strains of *There'll Always Be an England* came from the ancient gramophone. The officer with the red moustache clapped his hands sharply. The dozen or so *Kriegies* advanced to the centre of the stage and, linking arms so that they could high-kick, went through a grotesque parody of a chorus line, culminating in a desperate attempt to do a can-can, revealing the frilly knickers they wore under their skirts.

The ragged chorus line retreated and the blond young man in the silver lamé gown came forward, slowly and languorously, swaying his hips seductively as he advanced towards the footlights.

Slowly he raised his arms, thrust out his pelvis and broke into an amazingly realistic imitation of Vera Lynn singing *I'll Be Waiting For You In Apple Blossom Time*. Down below the German officer followed his every gesture with mesmerized fascination.

A plan was beginning to form in Crooke's mind. As the chorus came stumbling forward once more, he nudged Gippo. 'Pass it

105

on, let's get out of here.'

It was snowing outside – thick heavy flakes coming down as if God had decided to blot out the miserable war-torn world below. In silence, their collars turned up against the snow, they trudged around the circuit. Inside the huts the home-made candles were already burning; the Germans wouldn't turn on the electricity until the prescribed time so they had to make do with candles made from margarine and strips of their mattresses.

Crooke broke the silence. 'I guess that types like him will always be attracted to places like this. POW camps exercise an irresistible attraction for them – fit young men, cut off from women, and completely in their power, willing to do their bidding for a few cigarettes or a handful of food.'

'But how can we use him, sir?' Stevens asked.

'If we could get our hands on him, lure him here on a false pretext,' Crooke said slowly.

'You mean arrange a rendezvous between him and Kean?'

'Yes, something like that?'

'Then what?'

Crooke did not reply immediately. 'If we've got Suess, we're halfway to getting out of the camp. Perhaps escorting a working party out of the camp…'

'No go,' Thaelmann interrupted. 'There are no officer working parties leaving the camp. Officers – *and gentlemen*,' he emphasized the word cynically, 'do not work.'

'But there are dental parties going out every morning,' suggested Peters. 'One of my teeth was giving me hell last night so I asked a chap in the hut. There's no dentist in the camp and the *Kriegies* who are really in pain are taken down every morning for treatment.'

'But Suess wouldn't lower himself to take them into town,' Thaelmann persisted. 'The escort would be left to an NCO.'

'But he might see the POWs through the gate?'

Thaelmann nodded. 'That's possible. After that the "foot folk", the common soldiers, would take over.'

'We've got your "foot folk",' Stevens said.

'Who?' Thaelmann asked.

'*You.*' Stevens dug his big finger into Thaelmann's snow-covered chest.

'But where would we get the guard's gear

from, even if we could use Suess to get us through the first gate?'

'Would this be a start, gentlemen?' asked Gippo, and out of his copious blouse, he pulled a forage cap, decorated with the German eagle. 'I *found* this yesterday afternoon. It was lost, I am thinking.'

'You found it before it was lost, eh?'

Before Gippo had time to protest a figure blundered into them as it emerged from the latrines. It was Grey, the Escape Officer. 'Oh, excuse me,' he said, 'I didn't hear you in the snow.'

His fingers, attempting to button up his flies, stopped where they were as his gaze fell on the cap clutched in Gippo's fingers. In a moment his eyes took in the cap and Crooke could sense his mind racing as he digested the scene. There was a moment's awkward silence. The wind whipped the flakes against their immobile bodies. Suddenly Grey shivered. 'Bloody brass monkey weather out here,' he said. 'I'm off inside where it's warm. I'd advise you lot to do the same. On the diet here you get pretty susceptible to chills.' He made a play of shivering again and set off for the huts, his feet making no sound in the snow.

They watched him go, hurrying towards

the flickering lights of the huts. He disappeared round a corner. Although they could hear nothing, Crooke somehow had the impression that Grey had begun to run once he was out of sight.

the Reform Bills of the time. Dressing-
spread round a conservatoire, though they
could help walking. Ormiselewas
maintained that she . . . had begun to see a
admirals was out of date.

3

Over the next twenty-four hours the plan began to take shape in Crooke's mind, while outside the snow continued to come down in solid white sheets. His mind finally made up, he called the Destroyers together in the ablutions for a conference. While Peters kept watch for the goons at the door, they arranged themselves over their washing on the rear row with the taps running to drown their voices.

'As you all know,' Crooke started, 'the first principle of any good commander is to attack the enemy at his weakest point. In this camp, however, it seems to me, escapers so far have always tackled the camp's strongest point. In daytime there are thirty feet of no-man's-land to be crossed before you can get to the wire and all that time the goons can fire. At night it's well lit and patrolled. In short, the first wire fence is the Germans' front line. If you ask me I'd say the Germans' weak spot is the second and third fences. The men on guard there obviously rely on the men at the first fence to be doing the real checking. It's human nature – an understandable weakness.'

'Yeah,' the Yank broke in, 'but that don't get us any further. We've still got to get through the first fence.'

'Naturally, but I think I can see a way of doing that which will reduce the first fence to a weak spot and not the Germans' strong point. Instead of breaking out, *we'll break in!*'

The Destroyers looked at him as if he were crazy. Crooke put up his hand. 'Let's look at the original idea. We lure Suess in here, capture him and then force him to take us through the first fence under the pretext that we were going to visit the dentist. That would get us through the Jerries' first line of defence. Then what? We'd have to knock Suess out and park him in his office, because as Thaelmann rightly said the chief goon obviously wouldn't escort us to the dentist. So that job would be left to Thaelmann dressed in a poor imitation of a German uniform and with no pass if he were asked to produce one. At gate one and two then the Jerries would have us by the short hairs any time they decided to stop us. It's not on. I see the new plan something like this. We carry out the first part of the plan – luring Suess in here and the rest. Then instead of taking us all out, Suess takes out Thaelmann here, dressed in German uniform, at about four in the afternoon when they change the sentries. It's beginning to get dark then and Thaelmann's uniform won't stick out as it would in daytime if he were escorting us to the dentist. The two of them will move into Suess's office, as if they've got some work to carry out there. And that will be the end of that. After a while the lights will go out in the office and the sentries, who are after all facing into the camp, will think, if they bother to check, that Suess has gone back to his quarters. As soon as it is really dark and most of the traffic between the compound and the outside had stopped, Thaelmann works his way back to the wire and cuts it. If you recollect, the left edge of the Suess office-hut is only about three or four feet from the wire.'

'I'm reading you,' Jones interrupted. 'The idea's peachy. Nobody would expect anyone in his sane mind to try to break *in* to this dump. As you said, the sentries will have their backs to the outer wire. But as soon as our kraut here starts to burrow below the earth, even if he only goes in a couple of feet, to get to the wire to cut it, the seismographs would register his digging.' Crooke smiled. 'But he wouldn't be digging *below* the earth. Come on over here and I'll show you.'

The Destroyers trooped after him through the hanging underpants and ragged white towels towards the steamed up window. Crooke forced it open. Outside it was still snowing hard. 'How deep would you say that stuff is already?' he asked.

Gippo shivered. 'Perhaps a metre. That barrel,' he pointed to the wooden barrel underneath the pipe which ran from the washroom, 'is nearly covered.'

'Yes, just over three feet I'd guess,' Crooke agreed and closed the window again.

'All right then,' the Yank said. 'You said he won't have to tunnel below the earth.'

'No, he won't. He will burrow *through* the snow. A met man in my hut says the cold spell will last another forty-eight hours. So we can easily reckon on the cover of the snow for our tunnelling.'

'*We?*' Thaelmann queried.

'Yes. While you work your way to the wire and cut it for us, we shall be doing the same thing from – let's say the corner of the main

114

latrine. It's only about forty feet from the wire.'

Stevens dropped his towel on the wet board. 'Blimey, sir,' he said, 'I think you've got it!'

Only Thaelmann's face did not light up.

'The idea is excellent,' he said slowly. 'But how will you keep the direction under the snow?'

'I've thought of that. You will cut the wire directly to the right of the second post to the right of Suess's hut. There's a slight patch of darkness there – something to do with the arrangement of the lights.'

'But how will you be able to work to me?'

'By this,' Crooke said, as he lifted his leg on to the board and rolled up his trouser leg. A thin piece of lead piping was revealed, taped to his calf. 'From the washroom at the back, which is out of order,' he explained. He tugged at the tape. 'Here,' he handed the foot and a half long pipe to Stevens. 'Have a look at it.'

'Christ,' Stevens said, 'it's a bleeding periscope!'

'It's crude,' Crooke said, 'but it'll do the job. Half a metal shaving mirror at each end. Now we've got to get cracking and get the operation on the road – and remember we've only got forty-eight hours to do it. Without the snow, the whole thing's off, you understand that?'

They all nodded their agreement.

'So, let's get our fingers out. This is what we've got to do. We've got to get a message to Suess, purporting to come from Kean and luring him into the compound – by tomorrow afternoon. I've had a close look at Kean and even if he were told that he would be helping us to escape, I don't think he'd go along with anything which might make the other chaps think he was a pansy. I don't want anyone in here to know what we're up to.'

'I've been thinking about the message, sir,' said Stevens, 'and I've got an idea.'

'Go on.'

'Well, Suess does the censoring of the *Kriegies'* mail. How about smuggling the billet-doux in one of Kean's normal letters?'

Crooke realized the neatness of the scheme immediately. 'But how are you going to get hold of one of Kean's letters?'

'The post box, sir. A blind man with two left hands could get into the one in the corridor of hut five. The one Kean uses.'

'But won't Suess spot the difference in the writing?' Thaelmann asked.

'Well, it just happens that by – you might say – borrowing somebody's signature on a cheque for fifty nicker they sent me to Borstal. I think I could manage it, especially as friend Suess will be blinded by love, or something.'

'All right, Stevens, you're on. But remember we've got to have that note in Suess's hands by the morning.'

'What about my uniform,' Thaelmann said, 'if it comes off? And how am I to keep him under control once I've got him through the first fence? You know he doesn't carry his pistol when he's in the compound in case anybody jumps him – and I couldn't hold the fountain pen in his ribs when I'm through.'

Crooke answered quickly. 'Of course there's no time to make you a full uniform, besides I don't want us to get involved with the escapers' tailor. But thanks to the weather, you only need a German greatcoat. Gippo has already found us the cap, and a pair of RAF flying-boots with the fur lining pulled out should pass in the evening light for Jerry jackboots. So all we need is a German greatcoat which will reach down to the boots.' He paused and his brow furrowed in thought. 'An RAF officer's greatcoat, dyed, might do the job. But where the hell are we going to get a greatcoat? Most of the fellows in here have only got their flying kit and a couple of battledress blouses sent through the Red Cross.'

Gippo cleared his throat politely. 'I think I am possibly being of help there, sir,' he said.

Crooke knew Gippo's record and long fingers well enough; they had been the cause of his having been sent to the Cairo Military Prison the year before.

'All right, that's your pigeon, Gippo.'

'And I'll take care of the dyeing.' It was Thaelmann.

'I'm pretty good at whittling.' It was the Yank, who rarely volunteered for anything. 'I guess I could make a pretty fair imitation of a German Walther pistol by tomorrow afternoon if I put my mind to it.'

'Good man,' Crooke said. 'Then put your mind to it.' The fact that the Yank had volunteered, convinced him even more that his escape scheme was viable; the Yank wasn't a man to take unnecessary risks.

'But what do we do when we get into Suess's place?' the Yank asked.

Gippo answered for Crooke. He drew his long brown finger across his throat, making a rasping noise and thrust out his tongue as

118

if in agony.

'Yes, something like that,' Crooke began.

'Goons!'

It was Peters.

As he ran back into the washroom, they spread their washing out on the boards and began scrubbing as if their lives depended upon it, as indeed it might well have done.

A moment later the one-armed sergeant came in accompanied by Hauptmann Suess. As always, his pistol holster was empty and the flap open.

'The new boys, eh?' he said pausing at the door. 'Sorry about the soap. Not much good, I'm afraid.' He touched his peaked cap. 'But don't let me stop you, gentlemen. *Auf wiedersehen.'* He turned and stamped out, followed by the one-armed veteran.

Crooke waited till Peters reported that they had gone before saying softly. 'Now I wonder what that was in aid of?'

Two hours later, while Stevens posted himself next to the mailbox in Hut Five, Gippo stole into Crooke's room. He gave him a barely perceptible nod. Crooke got off his bunk and threaded his way past the card players and the distillers, busy heating their noxious bottles of yeast, currants and

119

potato-peel which they fondly hoped would eventually turn into something drinkable. The corridor was empty.

Gippo lifted the snow-covered blanket which he had wrapped over his shoulders. Below it was a fine blue RAF greatcoat.

'Good,' Crooke said. 'Where did you get it?'

'From that Air Vice-Marshal gentleman.'

'God, you mean Wing Commander Smythe?'

'Yes, that gentleman.'

It was too late to worry about Smythe now. 'All right,' he ordered, 'get it to Thaelmann and see what he can do in the way of dyeing it.'

Gippo disappeared.

An hour later, just after Crooke had finished supper, Stevens appeared at the door of his hut and beckoned to him to come out.

In the gloomy corridor Stevens pulled a letter out of his blouse. 'Got it, sir,' he said in a triumphant whisper.

'Fine.'

Stevens licked his lips hesitantly. 'A little problem, sir.'

For the first time since Crooke had known him the cockney was embarrassed.

'Well, sir, my old man buggered off with his fancy woman when I was ten. I didn't get much schooling.'

'You mean you want me to write the note for Suess?'

Stevens' face brightened. 'Right, sir.'

'Okay, you wait here. I'll nip back in and write it up for you to copy.'

Crooke went back into the thick blue fug of the hut. His mess had not yet received its weekly ration of cigarettes. As a result they were smoking home-grown German tobacco, bought on the camp's black market, wrapped in ordinary newspaper. The stink was almost unbearable. But Crooke did not notice it, nor the subject of conversation all around him. As usual it was food. 'Well, I say that we should eat the green hornets,' some-one was saying. 'They represent a valuable source of protein in my opinion.'

'Well, you can have my bloody share tomorrow night,' someone else commented, as Crooke started to formulate the little note.

'Dear Captain Suess, I feel that you and I have something in common.' He paused and bit his lip. He had not written a love letter since his wife left him. Now four years later he was writing one to a man! 'Perhaps in the midst of this terrible war, at least the two of us can do something to overcome the futility of it all. Would you please try to meet me this evening (Thursday) in the latrines – at four. Nobody's ever there then.' Crooke hesitated. Then he added the word 'please' and underlined it three times, telling himself that the word alone and its stressing should do the trick.

A few moments later the note was in Stevens' eager hands.

'Hope you made it sexy, sir?' he said. 'Get 'em randy and they can't see anything for the brown–'

'Go on, Stevens,' Crooke cut him short.

When the lights went out and the final *Kriegie* had dropped off to sleep with the tunnellers deep below the earth burrowing away in earnest futility like blind rabbits, the Destroyers slipped out of their various huts. Swiftly Stevens opened the door of the locked recreation room, where the amateur dramatics society met, with his crudely fashioned skeleton key. They slipped in after him and checked the blackout shutters before lighting the stubs of candles they had brought with them for their night's work.

Crooke had a quick look round. Apparently satisfied with their security, he said softly: 'Okay, lads, let's get down to it.' They needed no urging. Spread out across the stage, which offered the added protection of a thick curtain, both to keep their light from penetrating to the outside and the icy wind from coming into the unheated room, each man got down to his task.

Crooke, whose whole life since he left his public school had been solely concerned with war and the preparation for it and who had never been inside a factory, was amazed at the skills displayed by his men. The Yank squatting cross-legged in the yellow glow of his flickering candle, was completely absorbed in making an imitation pistol holster out of cardboard, marking it to give it a leathery grain before setting about the long job of rubbing it with boot polish to give it the right sheen. At his side, the guardsman sat, having taken over the white piece of wood, torn from under the Yank's bunk, which the latter had already whittled into the shape of a pistol. He had smeared it thickly with several layers of black polish and now with the aid of an old toothbrush handle and plenty of spit was 'spit-shining' it to give it the necessary gun-metal hue.

Gippo and Stevens were busily engaged in cutting up a piece of lino, soaking it in water and rubbing coat after coat of polish into it, preparatory to transforming it into a Germany military belt. Before them, a little pot was bubbling over a hissing Tommy cooker. It contained lead – and again stolen from the out-of-order washroom fittings – which would be formed into the belt clasp with its traditional legend *'Gott mit uns'*.

In the rear of the hall, in the little cubbyhole with its 'OO' sign, indicating the *Abort* or lavatory, was the only flush toilet in the whole compound. Thaelmann had already blocked it with huge quantities of cardboard from the Red Cross parcels. Now he was preparing his dye for the stolen greatcoat – a mixture of indelible pencil and green ink, again stolen from the Senior Officer's quarters. Soon, he told Crooke, who helped him to stir the mixture which would obviously block the precious toilet for good, he would be ready to start the long-drawn-out dyeing process.

The hours passed quickly. Outside the wind howled and the snow beat fiercely against the hut's windows, which was fortunate because it kept any goons inclined to prowl around the compound in their watch towers. But occasionally the eerie howl of the semi-wild Alsatians which roamed the space between the inner and outer fences startled them and served to remind them that even when they had overcome the guards, there were other, fiercer dangers.

Three hours passed. Four. Crooke started to glance at his wrist watch with increasing frequency. Time was beginning to run out. But there was little he could do about it. Each one of his men was working as swiftly and as efficiently as he could.

About four thirty, Crooke decided to go outside and check up on the situation. At the most he could give them another twenty minutes. If they hadn't got Thaelmann kitted out by then, they would have to call off the op for that day. Outside the snow was beginning to stop. But the wind still continued to howl and deaden the crisp crunch of his boots over its hard surface. He sneaked to the edge of the entertainments hut. Some sixty feet away the lights of the fence glistened icily on the snow. Beyond it he could see lithe shapes outlined against the whiteness prowling back and forth – the Alsatians. He flashed a look at the stork-legged watch towers. Up there he could see no movement. But he knew, in spite of their wounds and age, the veterans who guarded them were alert, their hands not far from the triggers of their Spandaus which would blast them to perdition if they made one little slip.

Crooke thought of their mission. The break-out was only the beginning. He still had to find the mysterious official who had ordered the death of the POWs from Stalag Luft III. Would he bite once they had got out of their present prison?

He realized that they would have to make their escape so dramatic, so harmful to the German cause that the killer would *have* to bite. He must be forced to take charge of them once they had been recaptured. Crooke forced himself to consider the possibilities of making the Germans hate the Destroyers so much that they would hand them over to the mysterious killer. Then he had it.

After being released from their preliminary interrogation, they had been taken by train to Koblenz. He had recognized the grim river-town on the left bank of the Rhine from a pre-war walking tour of the Rhineland during his first year at Sandhurst. He and Sandy Shaw, long dead in the desert, had walked the whole length of the Rhine 'just in case', as Sandy had remarked

126

grimly. 'You never know. We might be fighting here one day.'

From there they had transferred to the wood-burning truck which had brought them to the camp, and proceeded due west, deeper and deeper into the rugged Eifel border area. En route they had passed a lone German fighter base. The ancient guard in the rear of the truck had tried to force them into the interior, but he had been too late to prevent Crooke spotting the yellow and black signpost with the name 'Buechel'. If they ever got out, Buechel would be their target; then the Germans would have to take notice of them.

A few minutes later, chilled to the bone, he made his way cautiously back to the entertainments hut. He knocked softly on the door three times, the agreed signal. There was no answering sound. Softly he opened the door and crept in. His heart almost stopped beating. A German soldier stood there, hand on his pistol butt, his shadow projected gigantically in front of him as he faced the door, the yellow candlelight still flickering on the stage, though there was no sign of the Destroyers now.

'*Ach so*,' the German said maliciously, '*der

Herr Leutnant kommt auch mal nach Haus!'

Crooke's hand froze on his jacket pocket which contained the fountain pen-pistol. His mind raced. How could he get it out without the German shooting him down? But there was no need to. Behind the curtain there was the sound of suppressed laughter. The Destroyers staggered out, rocking with laughter, like a bunch of silly schoolgirls.

The German took off his hat and smiled. *'Guten Abend, Herr Crooke,'* he said and bowed. 'We fooled you, didn't we?'

It was Thaelmann.

4

'The fairy queen's coming,' Stevens whispered.

Hastily Crooke pushed him away from the slit in the planks of the latrine's wall.

Suess was plodding along the path the *Kriegies* had made in the snow to the gate, only the upper half of his body visible in the white waste. But even at that distance and in the growing dusk, Crooke could see that he was not moving with his usual vigour. His walk was slow and somehow hesitant; it expressed the hesitation and doubt that obviously possessed him.

Crooke took his eyes away from the slit. 'Right, Peters,' he snapped to the guardsman, 'nip round the back and stop anybody coming in here. If anyone wants to use the bogs, tell them they've got to go to the other latrine. If they won't listen, bloody well clobber them.'

'Yes, sir.' The guardsman hurried away.

'Yank, you do the same at the other end.'

He turned to Stevens and Gippo. 'Get up

129

in the cubicles at the other end and take Thaelmann's coat with you – and for God's sake, be careful with it. That dye will start to run as soon as you look at it!'

Stevens picked up the precious coat and disappeared with Gippo.

Crooke spoke to Thaelmann. 'All right then, it's up to us. Suess is no fool – obviously he'll suspect a trick. But his kind obviously have to face up to tricky situations like this all the time. He'll come in, I have no doubt, and he'll see you instead of Kean. But for God's sake, don't let him shout. Say something in German, that'll startle him, but his own language will reassure him. By the time he recovers, I'll have him.'

Thaelmann, as always, contented himself with a laconic 'Yes,' and squatted down on the wet unpainted boards, decorated with the obscenities of generations of *Kriegies*, while Crooke concealed himself behind the sacking partition of the next cubicle.

A moment later they could hear Suess's boots crunching over the hard-trodden snow of the path to the latrine. Suddenly the noise stopped. Crooke, crouching on the seat of the evil-smelling latrine, could almost sense the chief goon considering whether he should go ahead with the meeting. Suess knew how dangerous it could be for him. According to Thaelmann, homosexuality in the *Wehrmacht* was punishable by death; the Fuhrer was ruthless in his hatred of the aberration.

The feet moved again. Crooke held his breath.

'Flight Lieutenant Kean, are you there?' the German asked cautiously.

'Here, in here,' Thaelmann replied softly.

Crooke could hear the German's sigh of relief. The footsteps came nearer. Then he was standing at the door. But it was not the pose of the dominant Prussian officer, who knew he was all powerful, it was that of a nervous supplicant.

'Come on, come on, you bastard,' Crooke prayed, as the German hesitated at the entrance, peering suspiciously into the gloom. Suess spotted the dark outline squatting on the seat at the far end of the latrine. He advanced down the corridor, getting away from the entrance where the sentries could see him.

As he got closer his pace quickened. Peering through his hole, Crooke imagined he could see a smile of concupiscence begin to form on his pale, plump face. Suddenly he stopped.

'But you're not Kean!' he stuttered, fear in his voice.

Thaelmann rose. *'Es ist schon gut,'* he said in German.

'Don't come close,' Suess said, 'don't–'

The rest of the sentence died in his throat with a strangled cry of surprise, as Crooke threw a muscular forearm around Suess's neck. With all his strength he dug his body into the German's back. 'Listen,' he whispered slowly and carefully, as Thaelmann hurried away to fetch the others, 'I'm going to release you in a moment. But if you shout, I'll kill you. Do you understand?'

There was no reaction. Crooke could feel the man's heart beating. Suess was scared out of his mind. He exerted pressure. Suess gave a stifled groan. 'Nod if you understand,' Crooke whispered. Suess nodded hastily.

Slowly, very slowly, as the Destroyers came running up the dark corridor, Crooke released his hold.

Suess coughed throatily, his eyes bulging with fear behind the thick glass of his horn-rimmed spectacles. 'What are you trying to do?' he gasped, choking on the words.

'Schnauze, du Schwein!' Thaelmann struck him hard across the face. *'Halt die Klappe!'*

The German reeled back, his fat face full

of shock and at the same time surprise that the other man could speak perfect German.

'That's enough, Thaelmann,' Crook intervened swiftly. 'We don't want his pretty face marked, do we?'

Gippo and Stevens took over. Before Suess had time to protest, their quick thieving fingers were all over him a pull-out his wallet, his *Ausweis*, the loose change in his pockets, tugging him back and forth between the two of them as if he were a live dummy.

At the same time Thaelmann, with Yank's assistance, was changing into his coat, while Suess's eyes grew wide with amazement, his thick wet lips uttering meaningless little sounds all the time.

'Now listen to me, 'Crooke said. 'Nothing is going to happen to you if you follow my instructions carefully. You understand?'

'I understand,' the German stuttered. 'But what are you trying to–'

'Shut your mouth and listen! You and our comrade here' – he indicated Thaelmann – 'are going through the main gate and from there to your office. You are going to walk through the gate as you always do. Do you follow me?'

Suess did not reply at once. He was like a

man trying to recover from a bad blow on the head. Stevens gave him a sharp dig in the ribs. 'Answer when the officer speaks to you!'

Suess said, 'I understand.'

Crooke took the pass which Stevens handed him. He tossed it to Thaelmann, now almost ready to go. 'That's his *Ausweis*. If anybody stops you, flash it at them and pray they don't look at the photo too carefully. But I don't think they'll stop you, seeing you're with the chief goon here. One last thing, Suess. You get our comrade through the gate and I promise you, on my word as an officer, that nothing will happen to you. But if you slip up, well–' he left his threat unfinished. Thaelmann, however, slapped the butt of the wooden pistol protruding from his cardboard holster menacingly.

Suess's face crumpled. Suddenly he burst into tears. 'Why did I ever come here?' he blubbered, the thick tears running down his face unheeded.

'*Schnauze, du Idiot! Willst du alles verraten?*' a harsh voice cut in.

The Destroyers spun round. There, standing in the doorway, was Grey, the Escape Officer, a big German pistol in his hand. He grinned when he saw the look of surprise on their faces, but there was nothing pleasant about his grin. 'Yes,' he said cynically, 'dear old ex-chief Clerk Grey of the Royal Air Force's bloody Volunteer Reserve!' He made a threatening motion with his pistol. They knew what it meant. Slowly they started to raise their hands.

'You,' Grey snapped. 'Suess come over here!'

Slowly the German lowered his hands and walked past the Destroyers. 'Thank God,' he breathed gratefully, 'they wanted me to take them out of the compound... They were going to escape... Naturally I tried to fight them off...'

'Shut up!' Grey ordered. 'You were here because you're a damn fool and a queer to boot. And you'll pay for it later, my friend.'

Grey looked at the trapped Destroyers, a malicious little smile on his lips. 'It was easy, you know,' he said almost conversationally, but his eyes were wary, on the lookout for the slightest danger. 'Stevens there, hanging around the postbox in Hut Five and disappearing as soon as Kean had mailed his daily letter. That hat you had.' He pointed his pistol at Gippo. 'The strips of lino missing from the recreation room. Everyone in and outside the compound knows that lino is used for making equipment.' He paused and licked his lips slowly. 'One thing puzzles me, however, why you didn't approach me first.' His eyes searched their faces curiously.

'Because I didn't trust you,' Crooke snapped, 'and this has proved how right I was.' He spat on the floor. 'Because you're a damned traitor!'

'Ah, the one-eyed Squadron Leader Crooke,' Grey said easily, in no way offended. 'Not aircrew type really, eh?' He nodded to Thaelmann. 'And a chap who speaks German like a native...' He broke off, and stared at them thoughtfully, as if he were seeing them for the first time. 'You fooled that old buffer Smythe, just as I have done. But you don't fool me.' He jerked the pistol at them threateningly. 'What's your game, Squadron Leader Crooke – if that's your real name?'

'It's a question I might well ask you,' Crooke said carefully, his heart beginning to pound. The guardsman had appeared at the rear. Crooke had forgotten about him.

'I'll tell you what his name is.' It was Suess, a look of petulant rage on his tear-stained face. 'It's a very nasty one – that of a spy!'

136

Grey's grin of triumph vanished. Without taking his eyes off the prisoners, he said, 'You'll pay dearly for that, you lousy queer! We'll take care of you – but it will be slow and painful.'

'*We*,' Suess cried out. 'There you have it! *The Gestapo!*' Crooke felt a cold finger of fear trace its way down his spine. The Secret State Police! But he knew he must keep talking, keep Grey's attention occupied while the stealthy figure came closer, his hands outstretched to seize the Escape Officer's neck. 'So that's been your game all along,' he prompted, hardly daring to breathe. The guardsman was only five yards away. Surely Grey must hear him soon!

'Yes, of course. You British think that because one speaks your language, he must belong.' He shrugged. 'My mother was English and I spent the most miserable ten years of my life in your decadent country until my father brought me back to Germany...'

Then the guardsman pounced. One hand darted forward and caught Grey round the scruff of his neck. The other, palm open with the fingers clenched tightly together, came down violently into the hollow of his shoulder. The pistol rattled to the floor, where the Yank dived for it.

A moment later the roles were reversed and a pale-faced and shaken Grey was moaning softly, as he clutched his collar bone.

'Sorry,' the guardsman said apologetically, sucking his sore hand. 'He must have sneaked in while I was trying to ward off someone who wanted to come in here to pee.'

Crooke breathed a sigh of relief. 'Thank God you got the bastard, that's the main thing.'

'But what are we going to do with the sod?' Stevens asked.

Gippo pocketed Grey's wallet, 'Yes, what are we going to do with him now, sir?'

'Yeah, one kraut too many,' the American said softly, as he kept the pistol pointed directly at Grey's heart.

Crooke saw the point immediately. They couldn't leave him behind and they couldn't take him with them. But how could they dispose of him without alarming the camp? Suddenly it came to him. He could kill two birds with one stone. He swung round to face the chief goon. 'Listen,' he said, 'I promised you that nothing would happen to you if you worked with us, didn't I? Well,

I'm going to prove it to you. As long as he's alive he's a danger to you; you understand that, don't you?'

Suess nodded.

'So we're going to get rid of him for you. Then you'll understand that we mean what we say.'

'Don't be a fool, Crooke,' Grey blustered. 'If you manage to get out of this place with that queer's help, we'll get you again – and then?' He attempted a careless shrug, but it didn't quite come off. Fear was beginning to grow in his eyes. 'You can guess what my organization would do to you, if you harmed me in the slightest way. We have some pretty little devices in the cellars of the Prinz Albrechtstrasse...'

He broke off, his eyes suddenly wide with horror. Gippo and Stevens had followed the direction of Crooke's gaze. They had begun to pull at the loose unscrubbed board of wood which covered that section of the latrine. The Yank gave him a sudden push and he staggered forward. With a grunt Stevens loosened his end of the board. He straightened up and looked at Gippo still trying to free his end. The Yank pushed Grey again. Desperately he grabbed at one of the thin sacking partitions. It ripped and he

139

stumbled forward. Gippo freed his end and a nauseous odour enveloped them.

'You can't!' Grey cried in horror, *'you can't!'* He held his hands up in front of his face, as if he wanted to blot out the sight of the loathsome mess below.

The traitor tried to keep his balance on the wet duckboards, his eyes wide with horror. For a moment it looked as if he would save himself. But his feet slipped beneath him and he went into the pit with a scream. The Destroyers started back as the yellow liquid spurted upwards.

Grey came up, spluttering and screaming, his teeth suddenly a brilliant white against the nauseating yellow of the human ordure which stained his face and hair. Feverishly he tried to claw his way out. The Yank seized the long-handled squeegee the fatigue men used to clean the duckboards and pushed Grey in again. He screamed and disappeared under the surface. He came up again with a squelching noise, the liquid dripping from his face, his eyes bulging out of his head with fear. Meaningless noises came from his lips, open like those of a fish on coming to the surface.

Behind them, watching the cold-blooded terrible murder, Suess was whimpering now like an animal in pain. Crooke nodded to Yank. The Texan took a deep breath. He raised the heavy squeegee above his head. With a crash and a snap of breaking bone, the squeegee came down on Grey's head. There was the smacking sound of suction. Slowly Grey began to sink. His shoulders disappeared. His head tilted forward. The liquid reached up to his chin. His eyes were still open and he was conscious, but he did not attempt to close his mouth. Bubbles came to the surface. For a moment, a pale hand surfaced, its fingers still jerking convulsively. Then it too disappeared. The surface of the pit was without movement. Wordlessly, Gippo and Stevens began to replace the board.

Ten minutes later Suess and Thaelmann had passed the gate without hindrance to disappear into Suess's office. Phase One of the escape had been successful.

5

Crooke gave an exhausted groan. As Peters squirmed past him in the icy snow-tunnel, he dropped their only tool, a blunt wooden board torn from his bunk, and began to blow into his cupped hands. They had been tunnelling for two hours but it seemed like two years. They had underestimated the resistance of the snow. Under the surface it had frozen hard and in spots it was as hard as rock. In front of him in the white icy gloom, Peters was hacking away at the snow, panting like an asthmatic old man.

Crooke crouched on his knees behind, shovelling the snow he cut loose between his open legs to the rear, where the others were crouched. He gave them five minutes, then ordered, 'All right, Peters, back up.'

Together they began to move backwards on their hands and knees, while the next team – Stevens and Gippo – took their places. Soon the little tunnel below the courtyard was filled with Stevens's harsh grunts and painful gasps for air. Another ten

143

minutes went by and Crooke gave the signal, 'Back up'.

At that moment the roof collapsed on Crooke. The snow crushed him to the ground. Summoning all his strength he thrust his hand out through the snowy mass. Awkwardly Gippo turned round in the narrow confines of the tunnel, gripped it and with a heave pulled Crooke free. 'Don't move, anybody!' he spluttered, spitting out snow and rubbing his frozen hand over his face.

The Yank and the guardsman behind him, about to clear away the fall, stopped immediately. Had the sentries at the gate spotted them? He forced himself to count sixty slowly but there was no sound save that of their breathing. The minute up, he thrust the crude periscope through the snow. The compound was pitch dark. No light came from the huts. Slowly he turned the periscope round to face the wire. The mirror gleamed a brilliant white. The light was reflected from the arcs hanging over the gate. But there was no sign of the sentries. He lowered the periscope. 'All right, lads, let's get cracking again. All clear!'

Twenty minutes later Stevens, who was at the front digging, dropped the blunt board with a stifled yell. 'Bugger it,' he cursed and started to suck his hand.

Crooke crawled up to him, his eye fixed on the strand of wire, protruding from the snow, which had caused Stevens's wound. 'We've hit the fence,' he announced. 'I'm going to see if I can spot the second post where Thaelmann has cut the wire. But no noise now. The sentries can't be more than ten yards or so away.'

Luck was with them. The second post was only five or six yards to their left and hurriedly they began to tunnel towards it. Ten minutes later they hit the cut wire and Thaelmann's deep furrow through the surface of the snow, which led to the back of the hut. Gratefully they clambered up into it. One by one they followed Crooke to the cover of the hut.

Carefully he raised his numb hand and tapped on the window three times. His fingers felt clumsy and twice their normal thickness, but Thaelmann heard the signal well enough. The back door creaked open. 'Good,' he whispered. 'Come on in.' They needed no urging. The wind was already beginning to freeze their soaked clothing. Thaelmann had got the pot-bellied office stove going and they headed for it eagerly, holding out their hands to capture its warmth.

Crooke stood with the rest, his purple hands outstretched to the glowing metal. Slowly the feeling began to come back to them. He swung his arms to get the circulation working once more and soon wished he hadn't. A sharp pain shot up both arms. 'I'll give you ten minutes,' he said to the others. 'Then we'll move on.'

He turned to the waiting Thaelmann. 'Where's Suess?'

'In the next room.'

'All right, let's have a look at him.'

Suess was bound and gagged in a heavy office chair beneath a large portrait of Hitler.

Crooke felt sorry for him. Whatever happened, the story was bound to come out. He was good as dead already.

With awkward fingers he undid the gag. 'Listen,' he said, 'we'll be off soon. Then you're okay. But I want one piece of information from you. Between fences two and three there are the dogs?'

'Yes.'

'How many?'

Suess shook his head. 'I'm never here at night. That was the dog handler's job.'

Thaelmann dug him viciously in the ribs. 'Think, you fat swine!'

'Perhaps one – yes I think one in each sector. The dogs have had some sickness. Two are in the kennels. I'm sure it's one.'

'All right. How are the dogs trained to recognize an enemy – by smell or sight?'

Suess looked at him in bewilderment. 'How do you mean?'

'Do the handlers use British uniforms when they train the dogs?'

Suess hesitated. But Thaelmann had no patience with him.

'Fat swine!' he hissed and whipped the back of his hand across Suess's face. Blood spurted from his nose and dripped on to his jacket.

Crooke sensed just how much Thaelmann hated those whom he felt belonged to what he called 'the decadent bourgeoisie'. 'Hurry up,' he snapped. 'We haven't all the time in the world.' With blood trickling down his chin, Suess said miserably: 'I think it must be smell. We haven't got the young men to train the dogs properly. The handler says you smell different from us.'

'You're bloody well right there, mate,' Stevens commented from the stove.

'Gag him again,' Crooke told Thaelmann.

He turned to the others. 'Listen, we haven't got the time or the energy for another bout of tunnelling. So we're going to try to cross the snow and get through the two fences as quickly as we can. There's one major problem – the dogs. But it's a chance we've got to take. Okay.' He pulled the bar of *Kernseife,* the ersatz yellow-white German toilet soap out of his pocket. 'All of you get in the back and start washing. We've got to get through those damned dogs and to do that we've got to smell like Jerries. Maybe the soap will help. Anyway it's the only thing I can think of.'

They crowded into the cubicle containing the washbasin, with its warning not to waste water and the neat black line to indicate how far it should be filled up. Crooke passed them the soap and they started to scrub away at their hands and faces like teenage schoolboys preparing for their first date with a girl.

Suddenly a long low howl echoed menacingly from somewhere in the outer compound – an Alsatian moaning at the moon. Crooke had visions of the half-wild animals the handler had let loose in the outer compounds the night they had watched the guards. In his mind's eye he saw again the dogs' permanently opened jaws and the vicious yellow teeth. The hairs on the nape of his neck stood up and he shivered.

Behind the hut, in the circle of icy white light, the inner compound continued to sleep. To the front, however, all was darkness save for the twin blue lights over the main gate. The Germans were observing the blackout regulations and the reason was obvious. A hundred yards from the gate was their own barracks, and they weren't risking having bombs dropped on their own quarters. The inner compound did not matter; it would be almost poetic justice if the Tommies dropped bombs on their own people.

'Let's go,' Crooke whispered, as they crouched in the shadows. 'We'll crawl. The snow's hard, but we'll give ourselves away if we walk on it. It'll make too much noise.' He hesitated. 'If a dog spots us, lie still and...'

'Bloody well pray,' Stevens interrupted.

'That's about all we can do,' Crooke agreed grimly.

One by one they began to crawl out of the shadow cast by the hut. The snow hissed under their weight and the icy cold penetrated their clothes at once. But the going was not too bad and they advanced steadily towards the next fence. Thirty feet, twenty, ten, the dark outline loomed up ever closer, the only sound now that of the protesting snow and their harsh breathing.

Suddenly Crooke stiffened. A dark shape moved out of the shadows to the left. It raised its head and sniffed the air. Crooke could see the movement clearly from where he lay on the ground. For a moment the Alsatian poised there motionlessly, as if it were trying to reassure itself that it had been mistaken. Then it turned and trotted noiselessly away.

A few moments later they reached the second fence. Crooke threw a glance at the main gate. There was no sign of the sentries and no sound save the barking of a dog at the far end of the compound. Crooke reckoned that the barking would keep the sentries happy; they would doze on, confident that the Alsatians were doing their job for them.

'All right, Thaelmann, get to work.'

Thaelmann crawled up, clutching the bottle carefully in his right hand.

The day before Gippo had stolen the

escaping committee's crude homemade wire cutters and Thaelmann had used them to cut through the first fence. It had been a long and noisy process. So, while he was waiting for the Destroyers, he made a thorough search of Suess's office for something more practical. He had not found any tools but he had discovered a large bottle of concentrated acid, which in its diluted form was used to clear blockages in the *Kriegies*' ablutions, caused more often than not by their habit of dumping earth taken from the various tunnels down the pipes. He would try and burn through the wire with the acid. Carefully, supporting himself on his elbows, he poured a few drops on the nearest strand of wire. The metal sizzled. To Crooke, alert for dogs and sentries, the noise seemed to take on the proportion of some huge frying pan filled with sizzling bacon. But at the gate no one stirred. The wire snapped. Thaelmann repeated the process. The next wire went and the next.

Hastily Yank thrust his hands into the snow and gripped the wire at one end. Peters followed his example, as a primitive form of protection from the acid, and took the other end. The two pulled the strands backward until they had made a hole big enough for the Destroyers to crawl through. Crooke watched them anxiously. 'All right,' he said, 'that's enough. Let's go.'

One by one they crawled through and began to head for a spot right of the main gate, where the stark bulk of the German Kommandantura building threw a stretch of the wire into shadow.

Crooke had just wriggled his way through when he stopped short. There was no mistaking the sound – the crisp pad-pad of a dog's paws over the frozen snow. An Alsatian was trotting in their direction. And this time the dog had spotted them for sure! The others froze in their tracks. The dog came closer. It stopped and sniffed the air. Then started to come on again. It was a great long-haired brute, with teeth that seemed too long for its vicious snout. Crooke's mind raced. One bark from the dog and the sentries would be awake, shooting at their defenceless bodies in the snow. He remembered the pen. Slowly and noiselessly he began to reach for it, but even as he did so, he realized that the dog would yelp with pain as soon as the slug struck it.

The Alsatian stopped and let out a low growl. Its ears sloped back against its skull.

It bared its long teeth hideously, its wet upper lip curling back. Suddenly Peters lunged forward. His move caught the dog by surprise. His big hands snapped close on its jaw. The dog's bark was stifled just in time. It wriggled wildly. One of its great front paws came up and ripped across Peters's face. Blood spattered everywhere. The dog, which must have weighed eighty pounds, dug in its hindlegs and started to drag Peters forward, vainly trying to free its jaw at the same time.

Now Gippo grabbed the dog between the legs and squeezed as hard as he could on its sexual organs. Together he and Peters held on to the dog which had suddenly gone limp with the excruciating pain caused by Gippo's grip. Crooke crawled forward. The dog lay prostrate with pain. His fingers trembling, he placed the little pen hard against the pelt and pressed the catch. There was a soft plop. The Alsatian arched its body then lay still.

Five minutes later they broke through the last fence and Stevens had forced his way into the Kommandantura with his skeleton key. Together with Gippo he went through the rooms like a hungry locust. A bottle, half-filled with cheap German *Kognak* was pulled out of a cupboard. In another cupboard they found four greatcoats and four helmets.

'Put them on,' Crooke ordered. 'Thaelmann's okay and you too.' He nodded to Stevens who had taken Suess's greatcoat and cap. When they had completed the operation, Crooke looked them up and down. 'Not exactly a credit to the Wehrmacht,' he said. 'But come on, let's get on our way.'

'Where we off to now, sir?' Stevens asked.

'To blow up a Jerry airfield,' Crooke answered.

6

They marched through most of that night, following the usual infantry routine, fifty minutes' marching and ten minutes' break. At first Crooke kept them to the low volcanic, fir-covered hills which characterize the Eifel, but the going was too tough in the thick snow-filled woods, and he wanted to reach Buechel before dawn. So after a couple of hours of hard struggling which had them gasping like old men and covered with sweat in spite of the cold, he abandoned the hills and, trusting that everyone be abed at this time of night, took his men down to the roads.

To his surprise, the Germans had not implemented the rules of total war to the same extent as was the case in Britain. Street and road signs were still intact and within an hour he had a definite lead on the location of the German *Luftwaffe* field he had spotted from the truck which had taken them to Stalag VIIb.

The Destroyers were in fine shape. The

tough SOE training in Scotland had toned up their muscles again after the London fleshpots of the last months, but Crooke knew he should not ask too much of them; he must not destroy their last reserves of strength, which would be needed when they were recaptured. Without doubt Suess would start singing once German Army Field Security and the Gestapo began working on him in the morning. It would not be long before they discovered that the Destroyers had murdered Grey; and from what he had heard of the Gestapo their revenge would be vicious and brutal. At five thirty the horizon started to flush the first dirty white of the false dawn and on the ramshackle Eifel farms the cocks began to crow. It would soon be light and too dangerous to continue. They'd have to find cover for the day and try again the following night.

'All right,' Crooke said. 'We've got about forty-five minutes before it'll be…'

He never finished his sentence. His words were drowned by an unearthly noise as a black shape shot up from behind the wood to their front, red flames hissing from its tail. It roared upwards at a tremendous speed, faster than they had ever seen a plane fly before. A moment later all they could see of it were two thin red spots in the sky. A further second and it was gone altogether, leaving the still countryside to echo and re-echo to its tremendous roar. Slowly the Yank raised himself from the crouching posture which he had assumed instinctively and said, 'What in hell's name was that?'

Crooke shook his head slowly. 'Search me. But one thing is sure. Beyond those trees we'll find what we're looking for – Buechel Field.'

All that day they crouched under the firs which surrounded the airfield, shivering with the cold, but fascinated by the strange, black-painted aircraft, which kept taking off and landing on the place's abnormally long runway.

'What do you make of them, sir?' Peters asked Crooke.

Crooke who had been busy counting the exact number of the black planes, lined up with the conventional Me 109s and radial-engined Focke-Wulfs, shook his head. 'Obviously some new kind of propulsion. When we get back to the U.K. we can pass on the info to the boffins.' *'If you get back!'* a little voice at the back of his mind interrupted threateningly. But he ignored the little voice. 'That'll be their problem. Our problem is to get in there,' he indicated the busy field, 'and knock up as much hell as we can do so that it won't be back to the Stalag for us, but the concentration camp.'

Beside him, Thaelmann shuddered violently at the words, but controlled himself almost immediately. He said nothing.

'What do you mean, sir?' Stevens asked.

'Well, if we are to get the man who killed our chaps, we've got to make such a mess, stir up so much trouble that our activities are bound to be brought to his attention. Presumably if he was in charge of the killing last time, he'll be given the honour on this occasion as well.'

'A goddam strange honour,' the Yank said dourly, 'one that Mrs Jones's son could do without.'

'Now don't say that, Lone Star,' Stevens said, using his strange first name as he always did when he wanted to tease the American. 'Surely old Lone Star Alamo Jones ain't getting cold feet.'

'You know what you can do?' the Yank snapped.

'All right,' Crooke butted in quickly. 'Save your energy, you're going to need it. We

158

found ourselves in a few dicey spots in the desert. But up the blue we were fighting against soldiers and could expect the rules of the Hague and Geneva Conventions to be observed if we were captured. Here we're really sticking our necks out. When we're recaptured – and we have to be – it'll be the Gestapo and not the *Wehrmacht* we'll be dealing with.'

'Well, sir,' Stevens said, 'we ain't exactly been acting as if we was out on a Sunday-school treat ourselves, have we?'

'Sure,' the Yank said. 'What the hell can the bastards do to us? As that limey bastard there,' he indicated Stevens, 'always says – we can find and lose them before they know we've been and gone.'

'Good for you, Jones,' Crooke said. 'Now, this is the plan.' He snapped off a twig from the closest pine and sketched the outline of the field in the snow.

'Here's the main gate.' He poked a hole in the snow.

'The way we're dressed and without any weapons to speak of we haven't got a hope in hell of getting in there.' He dug another hole in the snow. 'That's the side gate with, as far as I've been able to make out, only two sentries.'

'So that's it,' the Yank said.

'Yes,' Crooke answered, 'and it's got other advantages apart from the obvious one. There's a lot of irregular traffic coming in and out there.'

'Yes, I've noticed that,' Stevens added. 'It looks to me as if the Jerries billeted in the village behind the hill use it and there's been a lot of vans there all day. Perhaps it's used for deliveries. You remember all the bullshit back at the depots. The front gate was reserved for the General. Joe Bloggs and his son had to use the back one.'

Crooke nodded. 'Besides the rear gate is closer to the airfield. But we still haven't solved the problem of getting through it.'

'Thaelmann could march us through,' Stevens broke the silence. 'Once we're through we could clobber the sentries and take it from there.'

'Are you kidding?' the Yank laughed.

'Yes,' Peters agreed. 'We're in shit order. We wouldn't fool anybody.'

The Destroyers fell into a gloomy silence. Regularly every few seconds the strange planes would hit the landing strip and then howl into the sky again and just as regularly the crows would rise in a great flapping flock, protesting hoarsely.

160

In the end it was poor shivering Gippo who came up with the solution. 'You have noticed that there are many vans coming from the village behind the mountain?' he said slowly, pointing a skinny brown finger at the church tower just beyond the hill.

'Bloody nice warm vans but driven by one man only. *One* – and we are *six*. In addition, we could get the van a long time before the camp. No one would see us drive in. No trouble with the uniform, no upsetments, nothing.'

'Yer,' Stevens said, 'but what kind of van do we nick? Knowing the Jerries, the drivers'll have to have a pass. You can't just pick any van. We'll have to find a driver with a pass.'

Gippo grinned. 'Simple. You spot a van leaving the camp. Knicker him, as you say, and then you are waiting until the sentry who checked has gone off duty. Perhaps two hours at the most. Then you drive back again.'

'So what are we waiting for!' the Yank asked, rising to his feet and brushing the snow off his knees.

'Nothing,' Crooke said. 'But, before we start, let's all get this clear. We're venturing into the unknown once we enter that camp.

161

What will happen when we're in there, God only knows. So we'd better get our cover story worked out and agreed upon now. We're RAF aircrew and we killed a German during our escape. Naturally we'll deny this. But,' he hesitated momentarily, 'they could make us talk, you understand.' He hurried on, as if he did not want to go into further details, but a glance at Thaelmann's face told him that he at least understood well enough what he meant. 'So we say we panicked and killed him. The result was that we knew we had to get out of the Fatherland damned quickly. Our only plan was one of despair – get to the nearest airfield and grab a plane. Unfortunately we picked on this place, which we'd seen from the truck bringing us from Koblenz. How were we to know that it contained a strange kind of aircraft that we did not know how to fly? What was left to us as patriotic Britons but to destroy as many of the planes as possible. At least in this way we were doing something for the war effort before – Hell, you know the rest,' he concluded hurriedly, as if he were eager to get the explanation over with.

'For the sake of the old country,' the Yank said cynically, checking over his captured pistol. 'Two and a half cheers for democracy – and all that crap.'

As they stepped back into the forest to circle the camp and reach the road to the village, Crooke felt a sudden pride in his motley bunch of old lags and killers; they wouldn't let him down.

They had three false alarms during the first hour of their wait in the thick trees on the side of the hill, which Crooke guessed would force any van to slow down into second gear. As they darted back into the trees two German Army jeeps passed, the men inside sitting stiffly upright like tailors' dummies. Hardly had they relaxed again when Peters, on the rock above them, waved to indicate that another vehicle was coming. But they had to wait a long time for the 'vehicle'.

It turned out to be a farm cart piled high with turnips, drawn by a plodding short-legged ox, driven up the steep incline by flicks of the farmer's whip. Crouched by a pile of neatly cut logs, Crooke wondered again at the contrasts he had come across in the Third Reich in these past weeks: on the one hand, technical perfection, dominated by brilliant brains, on the other, an agricultural system which seemed to have stepped out of a schooltext on medieval farming and the feudal system. In a way, he thought, a perfect war economy, providing tough infantrymen who knew how to accept orders and carry them out with unthinking, peasant purposefulness.

'Sir,' Stevens's voice cut into his thoughts. 'Peters is signalling again.'

Crooke rolled over on his side so that he could see the guardsman better. He was waving his hands – once – twice. Two vehicles were coming up the incline.

Minutes later a heavy truck lumbered by, packed with steel-helmeted robots, rifles clasped between their knees, as if they were going to the range to fire their monthly quota. It disappeared over the rise and sped down towards the village.

It was followed by the sound of an over-worked motor. There was the noisy crashing of gears. The roar of the ancient engine grew louder. On the rock Peters was waving his arms madly. Obviously this was the one they had been waiting for.

Thaelmann sprang into the road dragging a young pine behind him. It wasn't a particularly frightening barrier, but it would undoubtedly stop any unsuspecting civvie.

A moment later the ancient Opel *Wanderer* came into sight.

'*Halt!*' Thaelmann shouted and held up his hand in warning. '*Halt!*'

The middle-aged driver hit the brakes. He came to a shaky halt three foot away from the pine. Thaelmann doubled towards him, crying '*Ist alles klar?*'

'*Was ist denn los?*' the driver asked, leaning out of his window, gunning the engine all the time.

'*Ein kleiner Unfall–*' Thaelmann began, reassuring the driver while the Destroyers stole out of the woods like wolves.

Then everything happened very quickly. There was rush from all sides. Scared out of his wits, the driver let out the clutch. The Yank flung open the nearside door and grabbed him. The Opel jumped. Its engine died. With a grunt the Yank pulled the driver out and dumped him on the road in one and the same movement.

Thaelmann jumped behind the wheel, started the engine again. For a second he gunned the engine. Crooke pushed aside the pine blocking the road. This was the critical moment. If another vehicle appeared now, they would be caught in the open without a chance in hell.

Thaelmann rammed home first gear. The Opel shuddered up the hill and turned into the wood. He cut the engine and pulled the handbrake. The guardsman and Gippo started to pile up hurriedly broken-off fronds around the vehicle. Within five minutes it was all over; the road clean again and the driver, his eyes wide with fear, lying in the snow, Yank's bony knee thrust into his chest, a big pistol stuck under his nose. The Destroyers were ready to go.

7

The back gate was a piece of cake.

The Air Force *Obergefreiter* hardly glanced at the middle-aged civvie's pass. 'Evening, Jupp,' he said, 'you back again? I thought you'd delivered the bread for today?' In the back of the Opel, hidden by the canvas hood, Thaelmann dug the Yank's pistol menacingly into the baker's ribs. 'They called me by telephone. The sergeants' mess wanted some pretzels. They're having a *Kameradschafts-abend* or something.' He shrugged.

Slowly, observing the 15 kilometre per hour speed limit within the base, the German followed Thaelmann's instructions. A couple of times dark figures in *Luftwaffe* uniform loomed up in the blue light which came from the van's headlights, but the blackout had driven most of the base personnel inside their barracks. The place seemed virtually deserted.

As they came parallel with the sergeants' mess, immediately recognizable by the sound of hearty laughter and a thick beery odour, Crooke peered out of the back of the van. Blackness everywhere, save for the faintly luminous bent arrows and the sign *Luftschutzbunker* which indicated the air-raid shelters. 'All right, Thaelmann,' he said. 'Tell him to move on to the landing strip.'

'*Die Rollbahn jetzt,*' Thaelmann commanded.

'*Aber–*'

The protest was stifled by a grunt of pain, as the pistol thrust into his ribs. '*Schon gut, schon gut,*' he muttered and bore sharp left.

The van started towards the high, guarded fence which cut the landing strip and its strange planes off from the rest of the base.

'All right, Thaelmann, remind him that as soon as he's stopped by the sentry, he's not to say a word. Just slump over his wheel as if he's suddenly been taken ill.'

While Thaelmann translated the instructions again, Crooke turned to Stevens and the Yank. 'All right, get ready you two. As soon as the van stops, out you go.'

'No sweat,' the Yank said. 'After the past couple of weeks in that goddam cage, I'm looking forward to a little bit of a work-out on those Krauts.' He doubled his fist and spat on it. 'And remember no weapons to be used unless absolutely necessary,' he added, beating Crooke to it.

In the faint hue of the twin blue lights which marked the entrance to the field, Thaelmann and Crooke could see the steel-helmeted outline of the sentry, patrolling up and down.

He heard the truck. His slow turn in their direction and the casual way he unslung his rifle indicated that he was in no way alarmed. The van drew closer.

The driver pulled up. Casually but still cautiously the sentry advanced to the cab. 'Hey, what's this then?' he asked curiously. 'You been on the beer again, Jupp?' The baker's answer was to slump realistically over the wheel.

'Jupp!' the guard said in alarm. He lowered his rifle and hurried forward.

A foot thrust its way out of the darkness. He stumbled over it, fell forward and caught himself on the headlight. The guardsman's heavy fist clubbed him just where his helmet cleared the nape of his neck. His hands let go of the light and he slumped to the snow with a clatter of equipment.

Hurriedly the Yank and the guardsman grabbed hold of him and tossed him into the ditch while the baker stared at them in terror. Stevens doubled to the gate and swung it open.

'*Vorwarts!*' The van moved forwards. Hurriedly Peters collared the unconscious sentry's rifle while Stevens stuck the potato masher grenade in his belt. 'Keep moving,' Thaelmann snapped, as the driver seemed about to stop to allow the other Destroyers to get in.

As the truck rolled forward, first the guardsman, then the others swung themselves over its tailboard expertly and dropped on to the floor. The Opel drove on, past the long lines of Focke-Wulfs, tucked away in their hardstands, protected against air attacks by four-foot-high walls of sandbags.

'What about those, sir?' Stevens queried.

'No,' Crooke replied, 'if we're going to do the job, let's do it properly. We'll try for the funnies,' he added, using the name they had given to the strange howling aircraft which flew without the aid of props. He turned to Thaelmann. 'Just keep him going to the other end of the field.'

Two minutes later they halted by a line of the planes they had seen performing 'bumps and grinds' all day long.

'Watch the driver,' Crooke said and dropped over the tailboard. Swiftly he and Stevens walked over to the dark outline of one of the planes. The air around them was filled with a heavy oily odour, which was not that of petrol. He sniffed hard. It seemed more like paraffin, but he had never yet heard of an aeroplane which was powered by paraffin.

'I bet our intelligence boys would like to know about these,' Stevens said.

'I'm quite sure they would,' Crooke said, 'but at this particular moment our problem is how to destroy them. We can't do it with our bare hands, you know.'

'I've got the grenade,' Stevens said.

'That'd be all right for one, but its noise would have the whole place awake before we could do anything else. I want to take the whole lot with–' He broke off suddenly.

A yellow knife of light slid into the night, not fifty feet away. For an instant, it outlined the dark silhouette of a man. It passed away to be followed seconds later by the sound of someone relieving himself in the snow. The silhouette poised momentarily in the light again. Then it disappeared. The door closed with a squeak. The yellow light was cut off.

'Somebody taking a jimmy riddle,' Stevens said.

'There's a hut out there. Ground crew probably.'

'Come on,' Crooke ordered, making up his mind, 'let's go and look-see.'

They rejoined the others and ran quickly across the hard snow towards the little hut. A faint chink of yellow light escaped from one window. Pressed close to it, they could hear the sound of conversation from within. Crooke put his good eye against the gap in the blackout curtain. Four young men in their underwear, cigars stuck in the sides of their mouths, were sitting around a board table playing *skat,* while other *Luftwaffe* men, sprawled on their bunks under a low roof covered in pin-ups, were watching them intently. Swiftly Crooke counted them. A dozen at the most. He straightened up again. 'Stevens,' he whispered, 'give me the grenade.' Wordlessly the little cockney passed him the German grenade with its long wooden handle.

'I'm going in,' Crooke said tensely, feeling for the ring which armed the grenade. 'You Yank and you Peters, cover me. I'm going to try to blind that lot in there with science. If they kick up trouble, I'll let them have the grenade. Remember to duck.'

Crooke took a deep breath. 'Now,' he roared.

Peters smashed open the door with one

kick of his big boot. The yellow light flooded out. The Germans at the table dropped their cards. For what seemed ages, the two groups stared at each other, the wide-eyed *Luftwaffe* men and the dishevelled Destroyers crowded in the doorway. There was absolutely no sound save for the hiss of the gasoline lantern which lit the place and the heavy breathing of the men themselves. 'Good evening,' Crooke said in English. The words broke the spell.

One of the card-players reached for something in his pocket. It might only have been for a handkerchief but Stevens was taking no chances. He pressed the plunger of the fountain pen. The card-player screamed and pitched forward over the table. The table rocked and overturned, sending greasy cards flying. Another card-player rose to his feet, shouting angrily. Peters drove the butt of his rifle into his face. Blood spurted from the man's broken nose. He sat down abruptly, his hands cradling his face.

'*Du Schwein!*' a bespectacled studious-looking *Luftwaffe* man on one of the bunks cried. The Yank grabbed him by the naked leg and twisted hard. The German crashed to the floor on his face and his glasses shattered.

For a moment the barrack room was complete confusion, filled with struggling cursing men, swaying back and forth in hand-to-hand combat, while Crooke stood to one side, grenade held helplessly in his raised fist; he could not use it now without endangering his own men.

Suddenly Thaelmann's harsh voice cut into the fight with Prussian authority. 'We are British paras,' he yelled. 'All resistance is foolish. The whole field is in our hands! *Drop your weapons now, if you want to live!*'

The authoritative voice in their own language and the mention of the paras had their effect. The *Luftwaffe* men dropped the bottles they had seized. Thaelmann, standing at the door, gestured threateningly with the pistol. One after another the Germans began to raise their hands.

Stevens and Gippo went through the hut like two human locusts. Quickly they discovered what was probably the crew's meal for the night shift – packets of thick black bread sandwiches covered in *Leber-wurst*. Stevens tore open the paper and started slinging sandwiches to the starved Destroyers.

But it was Gippo who solved the problem of what to do with the strange planes. In the little room off the sleeping quarter he found the crew's weapons – and a box of British Mills bombs, probably taken at Dunkirk or even at Dieppe.

Thaelmann ordered the Germans to begin arming the grenades. They hesitated, but a vicious kick between the legs sent one of them whimpering to the floor and did the trick.

'That's the only way with krauts,' Yank said. Hurriedly the Germans began to carry out Thaelmann's orders.

A moon had come up. The planes stood out starkly in its light. They looked strangely beautiful, Crooke thought. Sleek, deadly, all-powerful in the air, but now completely impotent – at their mercy; and each the result of thousands of pounds of painful craftsmanship, now to be destroyed in seconds by the murderous little eggs in their hands.

'All right,' he said. 'Remember you've got four seconds time-lag once you've placed the bomb. So get your skates on!'

Cockpit open, pin out, bomb inside and run like hell. The first plane went up in a sheet of flame. Its undercarriage gave way and it slumped like a broken-legged bird.

Then the second one exploded. The grenade must have caught its fuel tank, too. It went up in a much more violent explosion. Plane after plane went up in flames, while far away on the other side of the field the sirens began to wail and there was the throaty cough of engines getting off to a cold start.

Crooke panted after the rest. Cockpit open, pin out, bomb in, drop and run. In spite of the freezing cold, his face was lathered in sweat, coloured a ruddy hue by the burning planes. The Yank, who had run out of grenades, was firing shot after shot into the fuel tanks of a plane fifteen feet away. Behind, the siren was rising to a crescendo. The roar of the trucks was getting ever closer. Fingers of light were probing the darkness. Searchlights.

Then they heard the first shots. Single, hesitant, unaimed. They were followed by the chatter of a heavy machine-gun. Red tracer stitched across the blackness. *'Hier druben ... hier druben!'* a voice close by called hoarsely.

Crooke knew what must come now. A white light flicked on. Blinded, he raised his hands and tried to protect his face. Something smashed into his stomach and he crashed heavily to the ground, the breath

176

knocked out of him. Instinctively he rolled himself into the foetal position. Not a moment too soon. The heavy studded boots started to crush into his body – over and over again.

SECTION THREE:
NACHT UND NEBEL★

'Everyone here sells everyone. A piece of bread as a reward is enough.'

Unknown Concentration Camp inmate to Lt. Crooke.

★Gestapo expression for prisoners to be imprisoned and finally executed without trial or trace.

1

'Terrorist ... englisches Schwein ... Mistkerl....!'
The cries seemed to come from far away, but there was no mistaking their hate and rage.

Crooke shook his head. It felt twice its normal size. Slowly the mist began to clear. He wiped the back of his hand across his face. It was wet. He stared down at his hand. It was covered with blood.

Gradually his eyes focused to take in a high bare room, the standard picture of Hitler behind the desk in the corner. Through the barred window he saw two grey steeples.

'Viktor!' the same harsh voice, which had woken him cried angrily.

A broad-shouldered man with the brick-red face of a heavy drinker stepped into Crooke's vision. He spat in the tied-up Destroyer's face and gave him a crashing slap which sent him and the chair careering against the wall. Viktor followed him. His heavy boot crashed into Crooke's side.

Crooke let his body go limp to minimize the effect of the kicks. The kicking seemed to go on for ever.

'All right, Viktor,' the harsh voice said in English, 'that's enough.'

Viktor reached down and pulled the chair upright. He put another chair in front of Crooke and stood to attention by his side.

For a moment nothing happened. Then something moved out of the shadow in the corner of the room. A tall emaciated man stepped into the light. In spite of the grey-green uniform he was wearing, Crooke knew instinctively that he was not a soldier. There was something about him which, allied to his cold grey eyes and narrow rat-trap of a mouth, stamped him as one thing only – a Gestapo man.

The tall man swung his leg over the chair and stared at Crooke with expressionless eyes. He hauled back his fist. Crooke caught the gleam of a big blue and yellow ring on his clenched fist. The fist crashed into the centre of his face. Crooke's glass eye shot out and clattered to the floor.

The tall man's face remained completely expressionless. Without looking down, he flicked the eye away with the tip of his highly polished jackboot. 'Now you know where you stand, you British swine,' he said drily, without any emotion in his voice. He licked his lips and slowly massaged his hand. 'My name is Doerr – *Obersturmbannführer Doerr,*' he continued, never taking his eyes from Crooke's battered face, 'and I am going to make you talk. *Understand?*' Again the fist crashed into Crooke's face. His lips split like a burst plum. But Doerr did not even seem to notice. He went on in the same harsh dry way. 'I am going to ask you three questions, which you will answer. Where is Grey? What did you know about the *Duesenjaeger?* What is your mission?'

In spite of the pain Crooke made a conscious effort to imprint the word *Duesenjaeger* on his memory. 'I am not telling you anything. I am a British officer protected by the Geneva...'

'Viktor!' Doerr shouted.

Viktor clenched his fist and brought it down like a club on the nape of Crooke's neck. Crooke screamed. Viktor hit him again. Doerr crashed his fist in Crooke's face. Then like two boxers working out on a punchbag in some backstreet gym, the two of them began to beat up the helpless officer, the silence broken only by their heavy breathing and the faint mocking

183

sound of church bells from outside.

His mouth full of blood, his face puffed up to the shape of a balloon, Crooke let his head fall as if he had fallen unconscious, which was not far from the truth. They struck him a couple of times more and gave up.

'*Arschloch*,' Viktor grunted. He seized Crooke by the hair and held up his face. It took Crooke all his willpower to stop himself from screaming with pain. Apparently satisfied, Viktor let his head fall again.

His head crumpled on his chest, his ears ringing with the blows, blood pouring from his mouth and nose, Crooke heard the scraping noise of a match, followed by the contented satisfied sound of someone exhaling cigarette smoke.

From outside the bells continued to peal, as if from another world. '*Verdammte Pfaffen*,' Viktor panted, '*mit ihrem Scheisslaerm!*' Viktor was complaining about the noise from the Catholic church.

Doerr laughed but there was no humour in his laugh.

'*Na ja, was erwartest du in katholischen Trier, Viktor!*'

So that was where he had been taken to. Trier was perhaps thirty or forty miles away from Buechel. He must have been un-conscious a long time after the *Luftwaffe* men had begun to beat them up at the airfield! He wondered where the rest of the Destroyers were, but he had not long to consider the problem.

'All right,' Doerr snapped in English. 'Give him the water!' A flood of icy water hit him in the face. Crooke could not help splutter-ing with shock. He opened his eye. Doerr was sitting behind the desk, puffing at a cheap cigar. For what seemed like a long time, he regarded Crooke's battered face in silence. 'Listen,' he said at last. 'I was a policeman under the Kaiser and I continued to be one during the Weimar Republic. Now I am one under the National Socialists and when they've gone I shall still be one. In short, Squadron Leader Crooke, I am a professional.'

The use of his assumed rank gave Crooke a slight hope; at least they had not got anything out of the other Destroyers. Their cover was apparently still good.

'And as a professional, I can tell you that it is no good trying to be obstinate. I shall get the information out of you sooner or later. I always do, don't I, Viktor?'

'*Ja, Obersturmbannführer,*' Viktor said in a

strangely sullen manner, as he clenched and unclenched his fist over and over again.

Doerr smiled faintly. 'You see, Viktor is growing impatient. He does not believe in my humanitarian approach. Well, let's get on with it. Squadron Leader, you've tried and you've lost.' He shrugged. 'Just answer my questions and then we'll see if we can treat you as an officer and not as a criminal. You see, your fellow prisoners have already told us all we want to know. All we want from you is a confirmation of their story. After all you are the senior officer.'

Crooke licked his cracked lips, on which the blood was already beginning to dry. 'What do you want to know?' he asked hoarsely. He knew he must gain time and find out what he could.

Doerr stubbed out his cigar eagerly. 'Now, that's better,' he said. 'Let us take Grey first.'

Crooke wet his lips again. 'He is the escaping officer in Stalag VIIb. You must know that?'

'Naturally I know that, Squadron Leader. But what happened to him? Suess shot himself as soon as the Lager guards released him yesterday morning. He made a bad job of it, blowing the side of his face off. He'll live – which one day soon he'll wish he hadn't – but he won't be able to speak again – ever. So all we have is you, Squadron Leader Crooke.'

Crooke knew he must gain time for what was to come. Even thirty minutes' respite would be better than nothing; it would give him a break, time to regain his strength. 'You'll find his body in the main latrine,' he said slowly. 'He's dead.'

Doerr looked at him aghast. For the first time he allowed some emotion to show on his cruel face. Then he picked up the telephone on his desk, pressed a button on the panel and began to speak rapidly.

'He was covered in shit when they found him!' Doerr said, putting down the phone slowly. 'Even his mouth was full of it. My God, what kind of a man are you to kill someone like that!'

'Du Saukerl!' Viktor smacked Crooke hard with his open hand. The blood began to ooze from his nose again. 'How could you do that! *Shit in his mouth!'* His face was flushed crimson. He looked as if he were about to have a heart attack at any moment. His whole body was trembling with rage.

In spite of the pain, Crooke was laughing inside himself. What a story to tell later – if there was to be a 'later'! Two Gestapo officials shocked by a killing. He realized with a growing sense of hope that he had discovered something important. In spite of their tough exteriors, Doerr and Viktor were not all-powerful. They had their weaknesses, their fears, like other men. No doubt they worried about their pensions, their bald spots, their kids, if they had any. Their present superiority was based solely on the fact that they were captors and the knowledge that their prisoners were frightened into submission by the very name Gestapo even before the torture started. As Doerr sprang from his desk and started to shout for the guards, Crooke knew he could win if he kept his nerve.

Crooke had a rough journey through the seemingly endless corridors of the Gestapo HQ. Every time he stumbled, either from weakness or because he could not see from the left side of his face, the two uniformed guards jerked at the chain tied to his wrist and it dug cruelly into his flesh. More than once there was the sound of jingling keys from up the corridor and the guards gave him a vicious dig in the ribs, crying *'Gesicht Zur Wand, Mensch!'* Obediently he turned his face to the grey wall to let some other poor wretch shuffle by. Crooke knew the treatment. Their SOE instructor had explained it to him; the prisoner was to be made to believe that he was completely alone in the world. A sympathetic look from another prisoner might bolster his courage; hence he wouldn't be allowed to see anyone but his guards – and torturers.

Further on they heard once more the rattle of keys ahead of them. *'Gesicht zur Wand!'* Crooke's guards yelled and pulled at the chain. Crooke did as he was ordered. The sound of footsteps grew closer. Two sets marching in step, the third dragging, as if its owner were badly hurt.

'Los mach man dalli!' he heard the guards urge on the unknown prisoner. The footsteps came parallel with him. Suddenly a thin but still bold cockney voice said: 'We're all right, sir. Tell 'em to go and…' Stevens's words ended in a thick grunt of pain and a gasp for breath. There was another grunt, followed a second later by the sound of something heavy dropping to the floor.

'Scheisse,' a guard cursed. *'Nun mussen wir ihn schleppen.'* (Now we've got to drag him.)

The guards pulled at Crooke's chain and they set off again. Moments later they marched down a brightly lit corridor, lined with doors from which came the chatter of typewriters and the jangle of telephones. The bigger of the two guards flung open the last door on the left and pushed him through. Inside the room was bare save for a big bath set into the floor.

Outside there were hoarse shouts, followed by the clatter of high heels. A crowd of secretaries in short, flowered dresses and high wooden shoes, filled the open doorway behind him. Some shivered at the appearance of the one-eyed officer. Others giggled nervously. Doerr forced his way through them with a polite, if fake, *'Entschuldigen Sie, meine Damen.'* He was followed by Viktor.

'Get his pants off,' he snapped at one of the guards.

The man released his hold on the chain. While Crooke wriggled vainly, he pulled off his trousers, then his underpants.

A couple of the girls shrieked and hid their faces in their hands. One of the older ones jeered. 'Look at that poor little thing!'

Viktor grabbed him by the scruff of the neck and bent him down to face the bath. 'Are you going to talk now?'

'No,' Crooke said weakly.

'Good,' Doerr ordered. 'Fill it up.'

While Crooke, held firmly in Viktor's grasp, watched with horrified fascination, the bath started to fill with water. When Viktor was satisfied that the water was deep enough he signalled to one of the guards to turn the water off and forced Crooke's head down into the bath. Crooke panicked. With all his strength he kicked out. But Viktor was expecting the kick. He had his legs open. Crooke's foot struck the air. The next moment someone grabbed his feet. He was powerless to move now. His mouth came open. He swallowed water. His lungs seemed about to burst. Desperately he struggled to free himself from the vice-like grip on his neck and legs. A great roar began in his ears. The thick heavy blackness started to descend upon him. He was drowning.

Crooke came to. The angry voices seemed miles away. He gasped greedily for air. An agonizing pain shot through his chest. Suddenly he vomited. Water gushed from his mouth and splashed onto the floor in front of Viktor's polished boots. *'Du Schwein!'* Viktor cursed and kicked him in the side.

The black haze which had gathered around his eye vanished. He vomited again on the floor.

Behind him at the door one of the secretaries began to cry. 'Don't hit him again,' she sobbed. *'Don't – it's cruel!'*

'Take them away!' Doerr shouted.

The guard ushered them out and the door crashed behind them. Weakly Crooke uttered a prayer of thanks for the unknown German girl; she had at least succeeded in giving him a moment's respite from the torture.

'Well,' Doerr said from behind him, 'are you going to talk now?'

Numbly, not trusting himself to speak, Crooke shook his head.

Viktor seized him again. The guard latched on to his legs. They flung him back into the icy water. His head struck the bottom. Violent red stars shot up in front of his eye. He screamed. But it came out as a series of bubbles. The air fled from his lungs. Frantically he tried to free himself. But Viktor's big hand held him under like a child. In a great gulp he started to swallow water. He came to to find himself sprawled in a pool of water on the floor of the bathroom. Viktor was pumping at his chest while the guard was pushing his legs back and forth.

'All right,' Doerr said, 'he's come round.'

Rapidly Viktor rolled him on his side. The water poured from his lungs. Crooke sucked in air gratefully. He could feel his heart beating as if it would burst out of his chest at any moment. His lungs sounded like a pair of ancient leather bellows.

'That'll do,' Doerr said. 'Get him to his feet.'

Viktor and the guard dragged him to his feet but his legs gave way under him. He slumped to the floor and sat there moaning, the water still dribbling from the side of his mouth.

Doerr looked down at Crooke. The icy look in his eyes had been replaced by one of bewilderment, as if he could not understand why this strange man was still resisting. Even in his extreme agony, Crooke realized that Doerr would never be the same again. By now, according to the code he had lived by ever since he had become a policeman so many years before, this man should have broken. They always did. But this one hadn't and he couldn't make out why.

The question would plague him until, as Crooke promised himself lying on the floor in agony, 'One day after we have won, I'll come looking for you. Then before I kill you, I'll explain.'

'Well,' Doerr said, and there was a strange uncertainty in his voice. 'Are you going to speak now?'

Crooke could not trust himself to speak. Face down on the wet floor, he shook his head stubbornly.

Viktor picked Crooke up as if he were a baby. Somewhere far off, Crooke could hear the door of the bathroom open. Viktor pressed him forward. 'Now, you bastard,' he said, *'drown!'*

Viktor forced him closer and closer to the surface of the water. In it he could see the distorted reflection of Viktor's crimson face. Behind it others too. Then he was thrust under. The great red roar filled his ears. In seconds he would be dead.

From behind Viktor came a soft voice speaking in English. 'That's enough. We don't want him to die – yet.'

As Viktor hauled him out and dropped him on the floor, gratefully receiving the gift of consciousness, his nostrils were assailed by the unmistakable odour of cheap perfume.

2

Viktor exchanged a few words with the SS sergeant at the gate. He handed him a piece of paper and the sergeant pulled off one mitten. Holding it under his chin, his breath fogging the icy night air, he scribbled something on it and handed it back to Viktor. Viktor, exhausted by his efforts in the torture room, beckoned wearily to the guards. They opened the door of the big black Mercedes and dragged out their prisoner. Supporting him under the arms on each side, his feet dragging on the gravel path that led up to the gate with its proud legend 'ARBEIT MACHT FREI'⋆ they carried him to where the SS NCO was waiting.

'*Nacht und Nebel*,' Viktor said softly.

'*Nacht und Nebel*,' the NCO echoed. He beckoned to the men waiting in the pool of light thrown by the arc-light on the gate.

Fearfully they hurried forward, skeletons

⋆ 'Work Makes Free'.

clad in striped pyjamas, with black armbands bearing the legend *Lagerschutz,* campguard. They grabbed Crooke hastily.

'*Nacht und Nebel,*' the SS NCO growled.

'*Jawohl,*' they bellowed, as if they were on some Prussian parade ground.

Viktor shook hands with the NCO. 'Good night,' he said wearily. 'A tough one, that.'

The NCO grunted non-committally. He waited until the Mercedes drew away and then cracked his riding switch against his boot. It was command enough. Followed by the NCO, they started to drag the unresisting Crooke through the outer camp.

The rows of long wooden huts were absolutely silent, starkly outlined against the winter moon. There was no sound save the soft hush of the wind which seemed to come straight from Siberia.

At his side the strange figures in the thin black-and-white striped pyjamas shivered in the wind. But Crooke was glad of it. After the heat of the car, it helped to revive him. He licked his cracked lips and started to take note of his surroundings.

Without a command, the pyjama-clad men stopped. They waited in silence while the NCO crunched past them in the snow and opened the door of one of the huts.

Noiselessly the strange procession went inside.

Another of the pyjama-clad shapes detached itself from the great green-tiled oven in the corner and came shuffling over to the NCO, rubbing his skinny hands expectantly. Unlike the men holding Crooke, he bore a red triangle sewn on his jacket and trousers.

'*Ja, ja?*' he said fawningly, staring up at the big burly NCO with the riding switch.

'*Nacht und Nebel,*' the SS man said.

'Good.' The little man with the red triangle nodded to the men at Crooke's side. 'Let's get it over with. It's long past midnight.'

While the NCO warmed his hands at the green-tiled oven, studying them as if they were somehow important, the pyjama-clad figures began to strip Crooke, depositing his clothes on the long table which ran the length of the hut.

Crooke was too weak to protest. He knew he could not stand another beating. He must conserve his strength. In spite of his ordeal in the Gestapo torture chamber, he had not forgotten that overpowering smell of cheap perfume. Did it have anything to do with the bottle that Mallory had taken off the dying RAF man? Or was it just a coincidence?

197

He did not have any more time to consider the possibility. At the table the little man had run his hands through Crooke's RAF clothing. 'Nothing,' he called dutifully to the NCO.

The NCO nodded and grunted something.

The little man beckoned in Crooke's direction. Slowly, naked as he was, Crooke walked over to him. The little man reached up and pulled the electric clippers down from the ceiling. As he did so, Crooke could see that most of his ear was gone. All that he had left was a dark-yellow hole and a piece of ragged flesh, which looked as if it had been chewed by some animal.

The little man flicked on the current and pointed to the three-legged stool in front of him. Crooke sat down. Swiftly the little man ran his clippers over Crooke's head. Hair fell in a quick shower to the floor. The little man ran his skinny hand over the long tuft which he had left from Crooke's brow to the back of his head. He grunted his satisfaction and indicated that Crooke should stand up.

Before he could stop the little man, he ran the clippers over Crooke's pubic hair. A stroke to the left, a stroke to the right and it was gone. He straightened up again, his face expressionless, as if this midnight ceremony was the most obvious and normal thing in the world. His head concealed from the NCO by Crooke's chest, the little man began to shave him there. 'Listen,' he said in thick, but intelligible English, 'your friends are here. They came this morning.'

'Are they all right?'

By the stove the bored NCO farted loudly.

The little man jumped. Crooke could almost feel his heart throb with fright. He peered under Crooke's raised arm. The NCO was still studying his big red hands.

'Yes, all right, all right,' he quavered.

Crooke had never seen a man so afraid. His whole body was trembling.

He finished the shaving and switched off the razor. As he let go of it, it retracted itself up to the ceiling automatically. Then he walked back to the bench and beckoned to Crooke to follow him.

Obediently Crooke did so. He understood what the little man was about. Obviously he did not want the NCO or the other strange figures in the striped pyjamas to know that he could communicate with the prisoner. The little man held up his outstretched hand, palm outwards, like a traffic policeman. Crooke halted. He picked up a thick pot and a brush and again bent down in front of Crooke, his head concealed from the rest. In a whisper that Crooke had to strain his ears to follow, he said, 'Don't trust anyone in here – guards or prisoners. This is a dangerous place. The less you say, the better.'

Crooke yelped as the little man applied the first stroke of the brush to his hairless genitals.

A strong medical smell filled the air and the NCO looked across at them lazily. He yawned and turned to the stove again.

'Medicine against the lice. Typhus,' the little man explained hurriedly. Crooke looked down. The little man was covering the lower part of his body with a thick white paste. 'Everyone here sells everyone,' he whispered. 'A piece of bread as a reward is enough. Jews sell Jews. Germans sell Germans. It's full of spies. Say nothing.' He dipped his brush in the pot a last time. 'And for God's sake, don't say you are an officer. The Communists will sell you to the guards without mercy, if they know that!'

'What nationality are you?' Crooke whispered.

The little man looked up at him with cynical eyes. 'Nationality? Me, I'm a member of the master race – I am a German.'

He started suddenly, as the NCO bellowed. 'You, you little arsehole of a professor, hurry up, will you! I want to go to bed.'

'*Jawohl, jawohl, Oberscharführer.*' The little man put down his pot hastily.

Again he indicated that Crooke should follow him.

Together they walked to the far end of the room where a pile of what looked like rags lay, reaching almost up to the roof. The sweet-sour smell of death came from them. Swiftly and with surprising agility for a man who was obviously at the end of both his physical and mental strength, the little man jumped on the bench and started to throw bits and pieces of clothing at Crooke – a pair of holed cord breeches of the kind farm labourers wore in Germany, a French Army shirt, meant for a man three times Crooke's girth, a kind of forage cap, a pair of clogs and a tight green *Joppe,* with great holes in the elbows. Slowly and painfully, Crooke drew the clothes on while the little man hovered around him, urging him to hurry up, his eyes flashing back and forth between him and the NCO who was now picking his teeth in surly impatience.

As Crooke forced himself into the too

tight *Joppe,* a hip-length jacket often worn by German workers, with the little man tugging desperately at the front to aid him, he whispered his last question: 'The guard says *Nacht und Nebel* every time he refers to me. What does he mean?' The little man blanched. He did not trust himself to speak. His answer was to draw a bony finger across his throat just below his prominent Adam's apple. Crooke understood.

'By God, sir, are we glad to see you again!' Peters said eagerly, as the pyjama-clad *Lagerschutz* thrust him into the hut, filled from floor to ceiling with bunks, on which lay sleeping men.

'It's you, sir!' Gippo started up, his face, like those of the other Destroyers, covered with the ugly red marks and livid bruises.

'Gee, I thought you were a goner!' Yank said. Even he seemed to be concerned.

'Let me help you, sir.' The guardsman sprang from the bunk, with its wooden legs placed in four cans of water to prevent the bugs from climbing up them.

'Thanks, Peters, thanks a lot.' Gratefully Crooke allowed himself to be helped to the Destroyers' bunk in the corner of the evil-smelling hut. 'It's good to see you all again,' he murmured weakly. As if he were a baby, Peters placed him on the lower bunk and drew the rags he had used to cover himself and Gippo over the officer. 'Lie back there a bit, sir,' he said softly, while the others stared over his shoulder in silent awe at Crooke's battered face with the empty red eye socket.

Stevens bit his lip hard and looked at Thaelmann. There were tears in the German's eyes. Instinctively the little cockney knew what the Communist was thinking – his own people had done this to Crooke and he was ashamed. The Yank reached up to his tin bowl on the rickety wooden shelf behind their bunk, in which they slept two in a bed, and pulled out a hunk of dark bread, from which the straw ends stuck out. He placed it in Crooke's hands with surprising tenderness. 'Here, get that inside you.'

Crooke realized with a shock that he had not eaten since they had escaped from the Stalag. Painfully he began to swallow crumbs of the rock-like bread, helping it down with sips of water which Gippo brought from the tap at the other end of the hut.

They watched him in silence, like a

mother happy that her child is taking nourishment again after a long illness. There was no sound, save for the snores and the odd groans of their fellow prisoners, sunk in the only escape from the horror of the camp – other than death itself. Crooke felt his strength begin to return. The bread and water seemed to fill his stomach and send out new energy. But more than that, he was back with the team.

Stevens took a cigarette end from behind his swollen ear. 'Fag, sir? Only Jerry, but better than nothing.'

Crooke shook his head. 'No thanks.' He coughed and felt the stab of pain caused by a broken rib. He sat up carefully. 'Fill me in, please. Where and what is this place?'

The others looked at Thaelmann. He cleared his throat and Crooke knew he was in for a lecture. Thaelmann spoke rarely, but when he did he went on like a university don. 'We are in a concentration camp somewhere in the Saar not too far from Trier. And this place.' He waved a big hand at the sleeping hut, is the *Prominentenlager*, a camp within a camp meant for the *Prominenz*…'

'The big shots,' Peters prompted.

'Yes,' Thaelmann said. 'The big animals,

as we call them in German. The *Kapo,* the chief of this hut, whom you will meet tomorrow, tells me there are three hundred of them.'

'Three hundred – and six,' Stevens interrupted, 'with us. We're big shots too now.'

Crooke smiled faintly. Stevens had lost none of his old humour.

The Destroyers smiled too, happy to see him relax.

'True,' Thaelmann continued. 'Well we are the privileged ones, but out there in the camp itself are the ones the Gestapo does not care about. They have to get up at four in the morning and work all day on the same hunger rations we get until they are no longer capable and then...' he stopped.

'And then?' the Yank prompted, his eyes already beginning to bulge prominently, a sure sign that the shortage of food over these past days was beginning to have its effect. A month – two months perhaps, Crooke thought, and he would be no different from the sleeping skeletons all around them.

'Up the chimney,' Thaelmann answered, making a whirling upward motion with his forefinger.

'Pardon?' Gippo said, still ludicrously

205

trying to live up to his newly gained officer and gentleman status.

'The ovens – they burn the ones who can't work.'

Gippo shuddered.

'But don't worry,' Thaelmann hurried on, trying to reassure them. 'We're not for burning. The Gestapo wants to keep us alive – for a while. Besides,' he lowered his voice and cast a hasty glance down the hut. 'We have friends here – friends with power.'

'We?' Stevens queried.

'Communists,' Thaelmann explained. 'They run the camp. The camp police who brought you in, the man who cut your hair and gave you clothes – the clothing bull we call him, the *Kapo* in this hut. They are all Communists or sympathizers.'

'I see,' Crooke said thoughtfully, absorbing the vital information. 'The guards give the orders and *our* organization carries them out – if it suits them and doesn't endanger our own people. Most of them have been here for years. They have learned to survive. Because they have discipline and a cause worth surviving for. Some, however, are new here, the ones who came from the "Red Orchestra" – not the really big chiefs of course; they were executed in Berlin last year – but they are important enough, and brave. Mostly they're the ones rounded up in the sub-rings in Hamburg and Dortmund...'

'Hey,' the Yank interrupted, 'what the hell is the "Red Orchestra"?'

'I don't know much about it myself,' Thaelmann said, 'but in brief the Soviet Government started to establish an intelligence service throughout Europe in the mid-thirties.'

'You mean spies?'

'All right, spies, if you like – patriots might be a better word – who in every western European country were prepared to risk their lives in the fight against the fascist tyranny.'

Crooke wondered how Thaelmann reconciled his words with Stalin's Pact in 1939, which linked his country and Communism with the arch-fascist himself. But he said nothing. The Destroyers needed all the help they could get, regardless of its source.

'When the war started, members of the organization began to send information back to Moscow by radio and in the jargon of the *Abwehr** an illegal transmitter is an

*The German Secret Service.

"orchestra". This particular one was run by Communists, hence the organization became known by the enemy as the "Red Orchestra".'

'I see,' Crooke said. 'But what happened to the "Red Orchestra"?'

'In 1941 the *Abwehr* started to get on to it, as far as I know – on to its sections in the Low Countries. The lead there gave them a clue to the German section, or at least, the main group in Berlin. A year later most of the Berlin group was behind bars. Two months ago,' Thaelmann paused. 'Well, it was the executioner and his axe.'

Crooke remembered having read somewhere that important criminals in the Third Reich were executed by an axe, wielded by an executioner in full evening dress, complete with top hat, the victims staring up at him as he brought the blade down across their throats.

'The survivors here swiftly formed their own organization with the help of the Party. They have their contacts everywhere, inside and outside.' Thaelmann lowered his voice. 'Even among the guards.'

'The guards?'

'Of course. Who they are exactly, I don't know, but I'll find out. But there are those among the SS who are no fools, including the officers. Why do you think that they are in this hellhole? Because they don't want to go to the front and get their heads blown off. That's why! Now they see how the war is going they are preparing once more to save themselves from the débâcle to come...'

Abruptly a great echoing metallic voice cut into his whispered words. *'Achtung ... achtung ... achtung!'* It echoed back and forth across the outer compound. *'Die folgenden Gruppen werden sich in 30 Minuten beim Turm melden! Gruppe Kappes, Gruppe...'*

'The tower,' Thaelmann explained to Crooke. 'They're calling out the work parties for the day.'

The superhuman voice chanted on. By lifting himself on his elbows, Crooke could see the figures streaming out of their huts like ants answering the godlike call. Abruptly the outer compound was full of noise, jingling mess-tins, curses, blows, the barks of dogs – and above it all, that great voice calling its subjects forth to meet another day on the rapid path to sudden, violent death.

'It must be four then,' the Yank said and yawned wearily.

'Let's get some sleep.' Crooke nodded his head at the sleeping *Prominenz*. 'Besides we don't want them to see us getting together like this.'

'Yes,' Thaelmann said. 'You're right, the camp's full of traitors.'

'Good night then,' Crooke said, as Gippo sneaked into the bunk at his side, while Stevens, who had volunteered to do so, made the best he could of the hard floor. Swiftly he drifted into an exhausted sleep, disturbed only by great waves of sweet-smelling smoke that threatened to engulf him, only to be stopped at the very last moment by a soft voice whispering *'not yet ... not yet.'*

'My name's Radel,' the *Kapo* said in his rough but intelligible English, slurred a little by the fact that every tooth had been knocked out of his head. 'I'm your *Kapo*.'

He mustered Crooke, as if he were a sergeant major and Crooke were some frightened raw recruit. There was something very frightening about Radel. His thin lips looked as if they had never smiled, and below his shaven skull, his eyes were grey, cold and completely without mercy.

'Thaelmann has told me about you,' he

snapped, his examination apparently over. 'Why are you in here?'

Crooke looked over the man's striped shoulder at the shaven-headed skeletons shuffling around the inner compound, dragging their clumsy heavy wooden shoes after them, step by step, as if they weighed a ton. 'I suppose for the same reason they are in here,' he said.

The *Kapo* did not turn. 'Bishops, bankers, barons – opportunists, rogues, blood-suckers who have fallen foul of the man they once supported.' He made an irritable gesture with his left hand, from which the nails were missing. 'Scum, getting what they deserve.'

'And you?' Crooke asked boldly, knowing the great power that the man in front of him wielded, but knowing too that he must not show fear or he would be lost, 'what are you?'

The *Kapo*'s grey eyes glowed briefly. His emaciated chest swelled with pride. '*We* – not I – *we* are the people of the future. We are Communists!'

'Then we are on the same side,' Crooke said. 'We are fighting the same enemy, at least.'

'Are we?' Radel asked, but Crooke could

sense that somehow or other he had got over an unknown, unseen hurdle. 'But then Thaelmann speaks highly of you and the rest... You are not officers?' he added suddenly, catching Crooke off his guard.

Crooke thought quickly. All the Destroyers had had their uniforms taken off them by the skinny little 'clothing bull', as Thaelmann called him, and had been given ragged civilian clothes. But would the little man have been able to recognize the rings round the sleeve which indicated an RAF officer and if he had, would he inform the 'Red Orchestra' intelligence organisation? Crooke took a chance. He shook his head. 'No, all of us are sergeants. But why do you ask?'

The *Kapo* crooked a skinny finger at him. 'Come with me, I'll show you.'

In silence they walked through the pinch-faced frozen *Prominenten* who gave way respectfully when they saw it was the *Kapo*. They came up to two old men who were holding their frail arms to the crows in the skeletal trees beyond the wire, making twittering noises. The *Kapo* stopped, scooped up a ball of frozen snow and flung it at the trees.

Cawing angrily, the crows rose into the

sky. 'What do you think...' the words died on the two old men's lips when they saw it was the *Kapo*. The white-haired one took his peakless cap off and murmured, 'Good morning.'

Radel strode on, ignoring them. 'Fools then, fools now,' he said contemptuously. 'Trying to tempt the birds from the trees to eat!' He laughed suddenly. It was a bitter sound. 'That white-haired old fool was once the Bishop of Magdeburg. Perhaps he thought he was a second St Francis of Assisi!'

Crooke remained silent, overcome by the sheer naked hatred that came from his companion.

The *Kapo* halted and pointed to the squat black chimney on the other side of the wire, surrounded by heaps of white ash, which danced lightly in the air when the wind caught the tops of the heaps. 'That's the surest way of all, out of here.' He made the same spiralling gesture as Thaelmann had. 'That's the way the British officers, the ones who came two months ago, went.' He stretched his skinny hand through the wire and pulled up a handful of the ash. 'Dust to dust,' he said maliciously, letting it drift down slowly.

Crooke's nostrils, still blocked with dried blood from his beating in Trier, were assailed by a smell not unlike that of a classroom of unwashed children. 'You mean that's the crematorium – the ovens?'

'Yes. *Nacht und Nebel,* like all of us in here. That's the way most of us will go.'

'How many of them were there?'

Radel shrugged. 'How should I know? The oven's appetite is insatiable. It can swallow a thousand as easily as it can a hundred.'

Crooke persisted and Radel guessed the number might have been a hundred, brought into the camp at midnight when it was still asleep, not even 'processed', as Radel called the initiation Crooke himself had undergone, before being taken to the crematorium the following morning.

'You didn't see them yourself?' Crooke asked. At last he knew for certain what had happened to the escapees from Stalag Luft III.

'No, not with my own eyes. But we knew when they arrived and what would happen to them as soon as they were signed for by the *Rapportführer.*' He was the SS NCO who had taken him over from Viktor.

'How?' Crooke asked.

The *Kapo* looked at him coldly. 'You ask

214

too many questions. *Rapportführer* Finke works for us.' Crooke was impressed. The 'Red Orchestra' was obviously a very powerful organization indeed.

'Tell me one more thing,' he said after a few moments. 'Then I won't ask any more questions. Who was in charge of the guards bringing the British officers to the camp for extermination?'

Radel shook his shaven skull. 'It was not a man,' he said slowly. 'It was a woman!'

'Jesus,' the Yank exclaimed as they squatted on the hard snow and watched the life of the inner compound. 'A dame!'

'What else did he say, sir?' Peters asked, as they came closer to hear Crooke's account of his talk with the *Kapo.*

'Very little. Even his "Red Orchestra" couldn't get much out of the *Rapportführer,* except that she was in charge and coughed all the time.'

'Coughed?'

'Yes, as if she had a bad smoker's cough. Coughed all the time.'

'She ought to come in here,' Stevens said. 'This place'd soon cure her.'

Crooke smiled sympathetically and was glad again he wasn't a smoker. In the camp, the inmates would almost sell their souls for a cigarette. They made tobacco from virtually everything – weeds snatched from the fields while they were out on working parties, dried tea-leaves stolen from the guards' kitchen – anything. There were even Russians in the main camp who under the pretext of asking another prisoner for a light would touch the other person's glowing cigarette with what looked like a cigarette but which in reality was merely a paper tube; in this way they would suck up a lungful of the smoker's precious fumes.

'And nothing else?' the Yank asked.

Crooke shook his head. 'No, that was about it, except that the *Rapportführer* thought she was from the Cologne area – something about the way she pronounced her "l"s apparently.'

'But why do you think that this woman is the one we're looking for?' Peters asked. 'The fact she was in charge of the POW transport doesn't prove anything. Besides I didn't think that the master race allowed their womenfolk to get the top jobs.'

'Yes, you're right. On that evidence alone, there is no reason why she should be the person we are looking for. But there is something else. When the transport had gone, one of the Russians scavenged the area while he was waiting for his working party to move off for the day. He found this.' He opened his hand and let them see the little bottle with the picture of the horseman on it. 'He flogged it to one of the "Red Orchestra" Boys for a handful of daisy heads to make into tobacco.'

'It's the same as the one Commander Mallory showed us in London,' Stevens said slowly.

'That's right,' Crooke said, 'the one that poor young RAF chap had in his hand when the Dutch partisans found him. She's our woman all right.'

3

'The trick is to get into the other compound, sir,' Stevens reported, as they squatted in a patch of thin watery sun, a harbinger of the spring to come. 'In here they've got us taped. They've got our names – the lot. Six English blokes – forgive me, one wog and one colonial,' he smiled cheekily at the Yank, 'and a Jerry *plus* three Englishmen, we stick out here like a spare dildo in a convent. But out there are thousands of men from all over Europe. They look just like us. Once we're out there,' he pointed to the thousands of human skeletons shuffling around the compound, 'we become part of the crowd and as soon as we can, we go out in a working party. When we're outside–' He clenched his jaw and drove his fist into the palm of his other hand with a smack. 'I'll knock the shit out of the first SS man who tries to stop me.'

'Looks a snip to me,' Peters said, eyeing the single wire fence that separated the *Prominentenlager* from the other compound.

'Good,' Crooke said, 'but what's the situation in here?' He turned to Gippo whose job it had been to check the internal security situation.

'No problem, sir. The guards rarely come into the inner compound. Like outside, they leave everything to the *Lagerschutz*. The only time the Germans come in is for the *Appell* in the evening.'

'That's right, sir.' Stevens confirmed Gippo's statement.

'That big bastard of a sergeant with the Alsatian is the only one who has been in since we've been here.'

The Destroyers surveyed the misery around them and, beyond that, the horrors of the outer compound, where over a hundred men and women died each day, to be flung into the ovens like trash to be got rid of as quickly, efficiently and as economically as possible. According to Thaelmann, the trusties even pulled out the dead bodies' bridges and gold teeth to add to Himmler's treasure chest.

As if to emphasize the fact that human life had been reduced to the level of trash, at that moment one of the sub-humans in the outer camp bumped into a guard swaggering through the compound. For a moment the SS man seemed too surprised to react. A prisoner had had the audacity to walk into him!

The prisoner and the guard stared at each other in shocked silence, while around them the inmates drew back fearfully, knowing what must come. The guard reacted soon enough. He aimed a terrific kick at the offending prisoner. The man flew into the air, as if his body were weightless. As he came down, the guard kicked him again and then pressed the prisoner's head deep into the snow. While the other human skeletons watched in numb silence, the guard lit a cigarette, puffed contentedly and, giving one last press on the dying man's head, strode away, obviously pleased at having done his duty.

'Then there's the fence,' Crooke said, anxious to blot out the hideous scene they had just witnessed and get back to the job in hand. 'All we need is some kind of tool to break through.'

'It won't be as easy as that, sir.' It was Thaelmann.

'Why?'

'Look at Radel over there.' They followed the direction of his nod.

Radel was talking to two of the *Lagerschutz*

men, his shaven head close to theirs, as if he did not want to be heard by the other *Prominenten* dragging themselves by. 'Those are the guards for this compound. And if you went behind the huts, you'd see another couple watching the other side. Radel is giving them their orders – orders to watch out for anyone trying to make a breakout, though God knows why – none of these poor sods have the strength.'

'Do you mean, he's working for the Jerries?' Crooke asked.

Thaelmann shook his head. 'No, sir. He hates the fascists. But you see...' He stopped and stared around. In his day in the camp Crooke had learned the contemptuous name the other inmates gave to that frightened furtive glance – 'the German Look', a compound of cunning and fear. 'There is a radio transmitter here in the inner camp.'

'A radio transmitter!' the Destroyers echoed.

'Yes. But where it is, I do not know. All I know is the "Red Orchestra" is in touch again with their old director in Moscow.'

'But what the hell can they tell Moscow?' Stevens asked.

Thaelmann shrugged. 'They don't tell me.

But there are working parties who could bring information with them from the war factories – and in the camp itself there is a cross-section of the whole of Germany. A quarter of the inmates are German. There is a lot of vital information in this place, believe me.'

It was Stevens who, as usual, brought them down to earth again. 'Okay, so they're playing games with their boss in Moscow. But what's this got to do with Radel's guards and our escape?'

'Don't you see? Radel wants the *Prominentenlager* left in peace. He's in complete charge here. The guards don't interfere and he wants it to stay like that. But if six men escape – and English POWs to boot – then the Gestapo will descend on the place, take it apart, make arrests. Something like that would upset the boat. So he has the *Lagerschutz* watch us and ensure that we don't escape.'

'You must be joking!' Stevens said incredulously. *'Radel would shop us?'*

Thaelmann, a man completely without a sense of humour, said morosely, 'I'm afraid I'm not. He would if it suited his purpose.'

'You're a bloody ray of sunlight,' Stevens murmured grumpily and sank into a gloomy silence, in which he was joined by the rest, their hopes dashed.

Thaelmann waited a moment before he told him his other discovery of that morning. 'There is a way,' he whispered. 'One of the "Red Orchestra" men is going to try it tonight.'

Outside all was silent. Only a persistent dry cough in the pitch-black compound indicated that Radel had his *Lagerschutz* posted to keep any sleepless inmates away from the little equipment hut that bordered the wire near the ovens. Thaelmann had warned them that he would do so. Accordingly Crooke and Thaelmann had taken up their hiding places in the loft before the evening *Appell*, leaving the other four Destroyers to fake their presence in the emaciated ranks of the *Prominenten*. Now the two of them lay tense and hushed in the straw of the loft staring down at the strange little scene below.

While Radel watched suspiciously, the medic in the dirty white coat prepared the hypodermic. As he held it up to check its contents, his shadow flickered gigantically on the wall in the light of the spluttering candle. On the floor the 'Red Orchestra' man who was to escape looked up at him a little frightened. Not a word was spoken. The medic nodded. The *Kapo* grunted something the two watchers could not understand. The medic bent and slid the long hypodermic into the escapee's skinny arm. Slowly the medic withdrew the needle and indicated that the 'Red Orchestra' man should sit up. He dabbed the man's arm with a little alcohol from the bottle and then lifted it to his own lips. He took a deep drink and shuddered.

'And remember,' he said, 'when the *Rapportführer* checks tomorrow morning, tell him you've got lice. Understand!'

'Yes, I understand,' the other man answered.

'Thanks, Myer.' The *Kapo* shook the medic's dirty hand and he left, still clutching his precious bottle.

An hour passed. All was silent save for the soft tread of Radel's guards outside in the snow. Once the *Kapo* asked laconically, 'Anything?'

The escapee shook his head. 'Nothing.'

Another thirty minutes went by. Suddenly the sitting 'Red Orchestra' man groaned. Up above him, Crooke, still exhausted from the events of the past few days had dozed off. He awoke, startled, and peered through the slit in the floor.

'It hurts,' the escapee said, his face ashen gray. 'It hurts bad!'

Radel bent over him. The man's teeth were already beginning to chatter. In the flickering light Crooke could see that beads of sweat were standing out on his forehead. Radel pulled the man's shirt open and listened to his heart beat. 'Yes,' he said, as he raised his head again.

'It's working all right. We can go back in the hut now!'

He gave the other man his hand. With difficulty the escapee got to his feet. Just before Radel blew out the candle, Crooke could see that he was obviously ill – seriously ill.

With Radel's arm around him for support, the escapee dragged himself to the door. 'And don't forget the lice,' Radel hissed as he closed the door behind them.

Crooke waited till their footsteps were no longer audible, then turned to Thaelmann. 'What was that little performance in aid of?' he asked.

'The little medic – the drunk – used to be a professor of surgery at the University of Cracow. Rosenblatt's his name. Now he works as an orderly in the camp hospital for *Obersturmbannführer* Winkler, the chief doctor – also one of Radel's men.'

Crooke whistled softly. 'An SS man working for a Communist prisoner – that's something!'

'A turncoat,' Thaelmann said. 'A frightened opportunist out to save his own skin. But the escape scheme goes like this. Rosenblatt shoots the escapee full of some drug which raises his temperature and the like to give him the symptoms of typhus – it's endemic outside in the main compound...'

'Hence the business with the lice?'

'That's right, sir.'

'But if the chief doctor, Winkler, is one of Radel's men, why all the fuss and bother?'

'It's obvious. A German doctor would not lower himself to come into the compound to see a prisoner. Such things have to be reported before an inmate can see an *SS Ubermensch*...'

'Superman,' Crooke found the word for him.

'Yes. So the sick man has to convince the *Rapportführer* that he is sick – really seriously sick – before he can get to the hospital – for what it's worth.'

'Then what?'

'Fairly simple from then onwards. Winkler's men keep up the symptoms with further shots for a couple of days. Then the patient dies and goes up the chimney.' Thaelmann made the familiar spiral movement.

'But it's not the real patient.'

'No, just someone with his identity number sewn on his pyjamas. After all there are plenty of substitutes out there in the main compound. A hundred or more to pick from every day.'

Crooke nodded glumly. Thaelmann's words made him realize again just how close they were to death and how fast time was running out.

'What then?'

'The *Prominenter* assumes the dead man's identity in the main camp. There he's safe from the Gestapo, till starvation catches up with him. But in the case of the "Red Orchestra" man, he'll go out with a working party and won't come back.'

For several moments Crooke lay on his back and mulled over the situation. Naturally it was their only way out, but there was one catch – Radel.

'Listen,' he said at last. 'What chance have we of pulling off the same stunt without Radel?'

'None. Winkler might help – anything to save his skin. But not the medics, especially Rosenblatt. They all belong to us – to the CP. They take orders only from the *Kapo*. Without Radel, it's no go.'

'Then we must go to Radel.'

Thaelmann shook his head. 'He won't play. The escape route is reserved for his own people. He wouldn't risk compromising it for our sake.'

'All right,' Crooke said determinedly, 'then we'll force him to help us.'

'How? He's always covered by his *Lagerschutz* – and they are too many for you!'

Crooke noted the subtle change from 'we' to 'you', but he did not remark on it. He could well imagine Thaelmann's divided loyalties at that moment. For years he had lived the thankless life of an exile in countries which did not want him. The Eighth Army had imprisoned him as a traitor until Crooke had taken him from the military prison. Now he was back with his own people – German Communists – whose organization and discipline in the midst of the dog-eat-dog atmosphere of the camp must be a source of personal pride and justification for all those wasted years of exile.

'Then we must trick the *Kapo*,' he said slowly.

'How?'

'Listen.' Hastily Crooke explained his plan. It was full of holes, he knew, but there was no time for perfection. They had to get out, and get out soon!

Thaelmann did not speak at once when he had finished. 'But,' he said slowly, 'they are my comrades.'

'Of course,' Crooke said. 'But we are too! Remember the desert. But that's the past, I know. The future's important as well. If we don't get that woman, you know what might happen to the whole course of the war? And after seeing this place, I know that Commander Mallory was right. The Germans,' he caught himself in time, 'the authorities will not hesitate to massacre our prisoners if it suits their purpose.' He held out his hand. 'Give me the razor blade,' he said softly.

Thaelmann did not move. Crooke knew, however, that he had the blade concealed about his person somewhere. In the desert he had had it taped to the instep of his boot, for he had sworn that he would rather commit suicide than be taken alive by his own countrymen to suffer the terrors of Dachau once more.

'The blade,' Crooke repeated, his voice scarcely audible. There was no sound now save the squeak of the shed's timbers as they settled in the icy cold.

A hand came out and touched his in the darkness. He opened his palm. Something cold and sharp fell into his outstretched palm. It was the blade.

4

They pulled it off eighteen hours later. It was midday. In the camp the whole world revolved around half a litre of soup in the inmates' tin bowls. The thin lukewarm liquid was more important than loyalty, love, God.

'*Radel!*' Thaelmann burst frantically into the hut where Radel and his *Lagerschutz* were enjoying their privilege of eating their soup in the comparative warmth of the hut while the rest wolfed theirs down standing in the icy cold outside. 'The Englishman – Crooke! He's done something to himself!'

'How?' The *Kapo*, hardened to such alarms by nine years in the camps, put his bowl down slowly.

'Despair,' Thaelmann said and made a slashing motion across his outstretched wrist. 'He's bleeding like a pig. We must help!'

The *Kapo* got up slowly. 'The idiot!'

The men of the *Lagerschutz* looked at him over the edges of their bowls, each one holding his hand protectively around the tin container, as if to guard against possible thieves. Radel shook his head. 'No, stay there,' he said. 'Come on, Thaelmann.'

Together they hurried across the yard, filled with *Prominenten* swallowing their soup. They pushed open the door of the shed in which the two Destroyers had concealed themselves the previous evening.

Crooke lay writhing on the floor, clutching his left wrist from which the blood welled. A blood-stained razor blade lay in the dirt next to him. 'What the devil are you up to?' the *Kapo* cried angrily. 'That won't stop them putting you up the chimney...'

He didn't finish. Peters' big hand was clamped over his mouth while Gippo kicked his legs from under him. He came down hard on the floor, Peters still holding his mouth.

Crooke got up and wiped the blood from his wrist. No cut was left. The blood had come from a rat they had found that morning in the loft. He pulled out the pistol the Yank had whittled the night before with the same blade, and stared down at the *Kapo* whose eyes bulged angrily over the top of the guardsman's big, unwashed hand. 'I'm going to order my man to let you go,

Radel. But if you shout, I'll kill you without hesitation. You understand?'

Radel nodded.

Peters released his hold and Radel said angrily, 'Where did you get that pistol?'

The next moment he reeled back as the Yank slapped him hard across the back of the head. 'Knock it off,' he drawled. 'Speak when you're spoken to!'

'Listen,' Crooke said. 'We want to get out of this camp and you're going to help us.'

'How can I get you out? I have no...'

Another blow sent him reeling. He glared at the Yank, the blood beginning to trickle from the side of his mouth.

'The only way you'll get out of here,' he said haltingly, 'is feet first.'

'Right in one,' Crooke snapped. 'That's exactly how *you're* going to get us out.'

Radel flashed a look of hatred at Thaelmann. 'So they know, do they?' he hissed.

Thaelmann nodded. He did not look up.

For a moment there was silence. Then the Yank hit the *Kapo* again, hard. Fresh blood welled from his mouth and nose.

'Listen you commie bastard – we want out!'

Radel held his bleeding face, but his eyes were still defiant. 'All right,' he said thickly.

'You win. But one day, my British friends, one day...'

The plan went off smoothly. At first the *Rapportführer* looked at the six of them surlily when they reported sick the next morning. He was just about to wave them away when he caught sight of Radel behind him, his face yellow with great drops of sweat running down his shaven head. 'What, the iron man here too?' he sneered, but there was an undertone of surprise in his voice. 'Here,' he waved to the little bespectacled Polish doctor who did the first check. 'Have a look at this red bastard, will you? Perhaps our iron man is going to kick off at last.'

While the SS man watched with unconcealed interest, the dirty unshaven Pole checked Radel's pulse and temperature and gave a quick look at the *Kapo*'s yellow eyes. 'Lice?' he asked thickly in German.

Radel opened his palm. A dead louse lay in it.

The Pole started back. He muttered something in his own language and crossed himself hastily.

The SS man's mouth dropped open. 'What is it?' he asked.

236

'*Typhus!*' the Pole answered.

'Shit on the Christmas tree!' the burly SS man cursed.

'What the hell are you doing man? Get the lot of them out of here and over to the hospital!' He fled, leaving the terrified Pole to escort them to the hospital, the inmates shuffling out of their way as they staggered through to the outer compound, as if Radel and the sweating, ashen-faced Destroyers were lepers. Ten minutes later they were lying in the isolation ward, racked with fever.

For the Destroyers the next twenty-four hours were passed in a crazy, fever-racked charade. The orderlies would enter with a sheet, soaked in ice-water, and wrap it around their burning bodies to reduce their temperatures. After an hour the primitive treatment would begin to work, but just as the trembling mist around their glazed eyes began to dissolve, the immaculate figure of *Obersturmbannführer* Winkler would enter, hypodermic in hand. With a look of utter cynicism, he would press its contents into their arms and their temperatures would shoot up again immediately. Minutes later the orderlies would enter bearing fresh ice-cold sheets. The game would continue.

Once Crooke had the impression of someone tapping on the window opposite his bed. He raised his head painfully. For a moment a hazy vision of an officer in a sparkling black uniform shimmered before his eyes; then the fever overcame him again and he dropped back on the bed. Later Winkler explained that the figure had been that of the Commandant himself, ordered by Trier to check whether they were still alive. Winkler had told him according to his statement, that the Destroyers had only hours to live, and added, 'Thereupon the brave Commandant fled to make his report to Gestapo HQ as if the devil himself were after him. Surely such bravery should earn him another bit of tin to stick on his big fat chest!'

It must have been soon after the Commandant's visit that Winkler decided he should stop the treatment. Some time during the second night, when the primitive hospital, where, according to Winkler, his patients came 'not to be cured, but to die – as quickly and cheaply as possible', was quiet, he came into the ward himself.

The Destroyers' fever was over now and although they were weak, they were alert enough to keep regular hourly guards on

Radel to ensure that he didn't double-cross them. Winkler looked at them silently for a moment, before saying: 'It seems that my hand hath not lost its cunning after all. Verily you are cured. What, *Herr Kapo?*' He bowed mockingly at the tight-lipped Communist.

'You are *Obersturmbannführer* Winkler?' Crooke asked, his voice still weak, but full of authority. He spoke in English.

Winkler swung round on his elegant riding boots. 'And with whom do I have the honour to speak?' he asked.

'My name is Crooke. I arranged this. Radel had nothing to do with it.' Winkler stared at Crooke, then flashed an amused look at the enraged *Kapo*. 'So my man of iron is not infallible after all.'

'Watch your step, you fascist!' Radel snarled.

Winkler feigned mock alarm. 'But of course, my dear Radel! Of course. After all you are providing my ticket to the brave new world, aren't you – if the devil doesn't catch up with me first.' Crooke nodded to the American. 'If he opens his mouth again,' and he pointed to Radel, 'shut it for him.'

Crooke got out of bed and walked over to the German doctor. 'All right,' he said, feeling the strength coming back into his legs, 'let's cut out the nonsense, Winkler. You know why we're here?' The SS officer nodded but said nothing.

'Well, we're not just going out into the outer compound. We want to get out of the whole place. Have you found substitutes for us?'

'Of course, my dear fellow,' Winkler answered in an expansive fashion, 'a whole new batch of them. Any special tastes?'

Crooke ignored the question. He saw that beneath the SS officer's blasé manner there was a man filled with black despair and self-hatred. 'Good; we are going out tomorrow morning at dawn.'

Winkler accepted the news calmly, as if he spent every night talking to British officers who were planning to escape with his connivance. 'Considering the shape you are in, I suggest that you come into my private kitchen and get some food into you. In the paradise of the Greater German Empire outside, you'll find precious little, I can assure you.'

Ten minutes later, with Radel still under guard in their midst, the Destroyers were wolfing black-bread sandwiches, washed down with thin wartime beer.

Winkler smiled shallowly. 'Typical exquisite

German cuisine, famed the world over – sausage, bread and beer!'

The little hospital kitchen was silent save for the soft snores of the Destroyers sprawled out on the floor. Crooke, who was on guard, looked at Radel. He was sleeping too, his head slumped on the table before him. Crooke rose to his feet and crept softly through to the little office next door where Winkler was reading. 'What time is it?' he asked.

Winkler looked at his watch. 'Three. Another hour and a half before you should go into the camp. It's wiser not to get into the first groups. They are sent to Saarbrücken and Völkingen to clear up the bomb damage. They get the most guards, but of course there are more things to be "organized" in the ruins.' He made the same gesture of putting something behind his back to indicate stealing which the guardsman had used. 'The rest are sent out into the woods. Hard work. You get easily ruptured out there. Then you're finished.'

'Thank you,' Crooke said, puzzled by the man. Why should he care? he asked himself. Was it just to save his skin? Whatever the reason, the SS doctor's openness encouraged

Crooke to ask him a question, the one that had been on the tip of his tongue ever since he had come into their ward. 'Winkler, were you here when they brought the RAF officers here?'

Winkler nodded but said nothing.

'Did you see who brought them?'

Winkler looked at his boots. 'No, I concern myself as little as possible with those *Schweinereien*.'

'Do you know the name of the woman in charge of the transport?'

Winkler looked interested. 'A woman? Are you sure?'

'Yes, and I must find that woman.'

'Why?'

'That's nothing to do with you. But perhaps you can help me all the same.'

Swiftly he sketched in what he knew about the woman; her accent, the soft whispered voice, the persistent cough – and the perfume. Winkler listened to his explanation in absorbed silence, the hospital clock ticking away the seconds metallically.

When Crooke finished, he did not say anything, his face absorbed with some problem known only to himself. Finally he spoke. 'In the days long ago when I was a doctor, I used to pride myself that I could diagnose most normal complaints without laying a finger on a patient.'

'How?'

'Most good doctors can, you know. There are certain outward signs, which help. The redness on the inside of a hand, the colour of the white of the eye – oh, a hundred and one things. You, for instance, have what I call a "stomach face".'

'What do you mean?'

'Typical deep lines down each side of the mouth, allied with your leanness, which was there before you had the good luck to become a guest of the Greater German Empire. Hypertension obviously. If you haven't got them already, you will soon.'

'Got what?'

'Ulcers,' Winkler said, and smiled. 'But never fear, the Greater German Empire or the war will no doubt cure them for you.'

'What's all this leading up to?'

'The fact that the woman is from the Rhineland, plus her soft manner of speech and persistent coughing, probably to clear her throat, might indicate goitre. All along the border from the Eifel down to Alsace, the women have it. It is due to the nature of the soil – I won't bore you with the details. However, the constant use of scent does not fit into that particular diagnosis. Goitre does not smell particularly.'

'What does then?'

Winkler tweaked the end of his nose. Crooke knew now that Winkler possessed a keen intelligence. The problem obviously intrigued him and Crooke knew he would not lie, even though the truth would help the enemies of his country. 'Scrofula, or the King's Evil as they used to call it in your country and in France.' He raised his voice conversationally. 'In fact we have a professor in the camp somewhere who once wrote a book on it. A Jew of course.'

Crooke ignored the afterthought. 'But what is it?'

'A kind of tubercular complaint of the lymph glands, which in the old days people in your country believed the King could cure by touching the forehead – hence the King's Evil. Man is eternally gullible, you see.' He laughed softly. 'It was a good disease for working wonders with, naturally. The swelling of the throat and neck goes away at odd intervals as well as the other symptoms, of which the terrible smell is one. Thus the peasants thought the great man had cured them.'

'You're a terrible cynic, Winkler.'

The statement did not offend the German in any way.

'Would you not be in my place?' Winkler said, his voice suddenly serious. 'As a young man I saw my whole world fall apart. A few years later the great man came along, the saviour who was going to rebuild that world. And what happened? I end up here, a doctor who kills, not cures, and the great man sends a million young hopefuls to their deaths. But, mark you, for the cause, for that sacred, damned cause!' He shook his head, as if he were trying to fight back tears. He opened the drawer in front of him and pulled out a bottle. It was half full. 'Cognac?' he asked.

Crooke shook his head.

Winkler poured a glass, raised it and muttering, 'To the cause,' gulped it down. He put the bottle away again. His voice when he spoke again was completely under control. 'So, my dear Crooke. Whatever you are looking for this lady for, you'll recognize her by her hoarse voice, her emaciated condition – possible swelling of the neck – *and her stink, her utterly impossible stink as soon as she opens her mouth!*'

5

They dropped out of the rear window of the hospital, fifteen minutes after the gigantic metallic loudspeakers had announced the beginning of another day of misery in the *Lager*. Crooke was last to leave. Just as he was about to follow the rest, the loudspeakers began to broadcast music. 'What's that?' he turned and asked Winkler in surprise.

Winkler, looking as immaculate and elegant as ever in spite of the long night's vigil, shrugged. 'It's Carnival in the Rhineland. Most of the guards are local men; they're celebrating. You're in luck, Mr Crooke. They'll be in a good mood today.' He held out his hand. 'Can I bid you goodbye?'

Crooke did not take it.

'It's not dirty,' Winkler said but did not persist. 'In German, we have a saying, Mr Crooke – *Unkraut vergeht nicht*. Roughly translated, that means weeds don't die. I'll be seeing you – one day.' He turned and went back into the hospital.

Minutes later the Destroyers had split up among the emaciated inmates in their striped pyjamas stamping their feet in the icy morning air and clutching their 'grub bags', homemade containers in which they hid whatever they could find during the day. The guards, in thick greatcoats, huddled up against the cold, divided them into groups and with a few half-hearted kicks and cuffs herded them to the waiting vehicles. As their ancient bus drove through the camp gate Crooke told himself grimly that no one would ever get him or his men into that place again.

It was bitterly cold in the bus, but Crooke did not notice; his mind was busy with planning their escape. As the ancient vehicle lurched up and down over the frozen ruts on the little country road which led from the camp, he counted the guards dozing in their seats. There were six of them and another, cut off from the interior of the bus, driving. Seven in all, armed with machine pistols, guarding some fifty prisoners, huddled on the wooden seats. He looked at his fellow prisoners. Red-nosed and peak-faced, their teeth chattering with cold, they were already beat-sheep to be led tamely to the slaughterhouse when the time was ripe. But they would provide cover at least, if the Destroyers needed it. He nudged the American, huddled at his side, his face buried in the ragged collar of his jacket. 'Jones, are you listening?'

'Sure – and looking too,' the Yank answered.

'You've got the pistol, haven't you?'

'Yeah.'

'Okay, work your way to the front. As soon as the trouble starts, break the partition between the interior and the driver and get him to stop.'

'Roger.'

Slowly the Yank began to work his way to the front, moving from bench to bench, elbowing the skeletons out of his way.

Crooke glanced at the three guards on the back seat. They were still dozing. He beckoned to Stevens, who was seated with the rest of the Destroyers behind the other three SS men.

Stevens slipped from the bench, kicked a man who got in his way with his heavy wooden shoes and dropped down beside Crooke. 'We ready to go, sir?' he asked.

'Soon,' Crooke replied. 'Pass on the word. When the trouble starts, give the three in front of you this.' He made a gesture of pulling hard backwards.

Stevens knew what Crooke meant. It was a trick they had learned in Scotland from the SOE instructor. 'Will do, sir.'

'And tell Thaelmann I want him back here with me.' He nodded. 'Okay, that's it.'

The bus jogged on. Its interior began to stink of unwashed male bodies and the coarse black tobacco the guards smoked. Crooke rubbed a circle free of condensation on the window. They were driving through a shabby little village of tumbledown white-washed houses with great piles of steaming manure in front of their doors. A couple of elderly farmers were already about. They gave the bus a bored glance, then went back to their tasks. They had seen its like often enough before.

Soon the bus was passing through a wood lined with firs, their upper branches heavy with snow. This was the place. The snow would mean heavy going if they had to make a run for it, but the trees would provide cover. He nudged Thaelmann. 'Follow me.'

Crooke rose to his feet and nodded to Stevens, who held up his thumb in acknowledgement. Holding his stomach, his face contorted with pain, Crooke staggered to the back of the bus. 'Stop,' he moaned, 'stop the bus.' One of the sleeping guards opened his eyes. 'What do you want?' he said grumpily.

Crooke groaned and held his stomach in mock agony.

'He's got dysentery,' Thaelmann started to explain. 'You've got to stop the bus...'

The guard took his eyes off Crooke and turned to the German. It was the moment that Crooke had been waiting for. Instantly he straightened up and launched a tremendous kick at the guard's shins. He howled and bent down in pain. Crooke's knee came up and caught him under the chin. With a clatter of equipment his body shot back against the seat. He was out cold. For a split second the other two guards did not react. Then one of them shouted something and grabbed for his machine pistol. As his finger found the trigger, Thaelmann hit him. The bullets passed harmlessly through the roof of the bus. But the salvo acted as a signal for the other three Destroyers. As one they grabbed at the gleaming steel helmets of the guards in front of them and pulled hard. The SS men's helmets came off easily. The chin straps slid round their throats. The Destroyers did not relax their hold. Gurgling horribly, their frantic fingers fighting to relieve the awful pressure, their eyes bulging, the SS men began to die.

Crooke and Thaelmann had no eyes for the garrotting. They had problems of their own. While Thaelmann struggled with the seated guard for the machine pistol, the other SS man drew his sidearm. He dived forward, straight out of his seat, catching Crooke unawares. The bus braked violently and the two men fell on the floor in a heap. The Yank had carried out his task successfully. Crooke all too soon realized just how weak he was. Slowly but inevitably the guard was getting the upper hand. Crooke felt his strength ebbing from him. The gleaming bayonet was getting ever closer to his face. The guard pressed a knee into the muscle of his upper arm and the light of triumph glowed in his eyes. The knife came ever closer. Crooke knew he couldn't last any longer. A moment more and he would be dead.

Then suddenly the pressure was gone. The bus exploded in frenzied cries. Trampling feet were all around him. A score of skinny hands were tearing at the SS guard. Screaming with fear, the guard tried to protect himself but he was submerged by the skeletons, tearing, gouging, punching.

In minutes it was all over. The two remaining guards lay on the seats, arms outflung like broken puppets, their faces a scum of blood and bruises and their naked bodies a mass of scratches and lacerations, while above them towered the panting skeletons, their emaciated chests heaving with effort like a pack of hounds which had turned on their master.

Crooke got to his feet and picked up one of the fallen machine pistols. 'We've got to move,' he panted. He turned to the inmates of the camp and said in careful German. 'Leave the bus... Make a run for it – escape.' They looked at him in utter bewilderment.

Crooke turned to Thaelmann. 'Tell them in German what I said! Time's running out.'

Thaelmann repeated the message. From far away Crooke could hear the grinding of gears as some heavy vehicle took the sharp corner that led into the wood.

Still the prisoners did not move.

'You,' Crooke pointed a finger at a tall man minus one ear. 'Come on – let's go!'

A look of fear crossed the man's face. 'No,' he said and thrust out his hand stained with the blood of the guards. 'No, that's dangerous; we can't run.'

Crooke realized that the prisoners were lost. The blood lust which had overcome them and made them massacre the guards had vanished as swiftly as it had come. All aggression and energy had drained out of them. Now they were apathetic sheep waiting for the slaughter once more.

'All right,' he cried to the Destroyers, as the noise of the truck grew ever closer. 'We're off! There's no use bothering about this lot!'

The Destroyers needed no urging. They pushed their way through the silent throng of prisoners and dropped into the snow. A hundred yards away a *Wehrmacht* truck had skidded to a halt. An officer was peering out of the bus curiously.

'Spread out,' Crooke ordered, 'and head for the wood, *slow.*'

With his hands dug into his pockets he started to stroll casually towards the trees. The rest followed him, as if they were authorized to do so – perhaps to relieve themselves.

Suddenly a cry came from the front of the bus. It was the driver.

'Jesus, I thought I fixed that bastard!' the

254

Yank cursed, as the driver staggered into the middle of the road and began waving his arms frantically at the truck. *'Halt,'* he shouted and drew his pistol. *'Halt, oder ich schiesse!'*

'Run!' Crooke bellowed.

The Destroyers took to their heels.

A ragged volley of rifle fire followed them. At Crooke's side, the Yank halted, swung round and fired a burst with the machine pistol. There was a scream and they were running again. Behind them a machine-gun chattered. Lead stitched the snow all around them.

They ran on. The snow-covered firs seemed farther off than when they had dropped out of the bus. Bodies bent, their hearts pounding, they zigzagged, trying to outguess the soldiers sprawled out on the road. Suddenly Stevens staggered and fell. Crooke grabbed him and yanked him to his feet. 'Hit?' he panted.

'No, legs gave out under me, sir,' Stevens gasped.

Crooke kept hold of his arm. 'Come on,' he urged. More bullets whined past him.

'The sods can't help but hit us,' Stevens cried, trying to keep up as best he could.

Gippo clapped his hand to his shoulder

and yelled with pain. Blood poured through his clenched fingers. But he kept on running, the red spots on the snow marking his progress.

Crooke knew they wouldn't make it. They were weakening by the second and the trees were still ten yards away. His own legs were beginning to give way and Stevens was lagging behind again. He was on the point of collapse. The bullets sang through the air all around them. Ahead of them fir twigs flew wildly as the spandau's bullets stripped the trees.

Suddenly there was a great howling whoosh. A gigantic black shadow passed over the snow. Crooke stopped and stared upwards. As the plane flashed by and roared into the sky, he caught a glimpse of twin white stars. *The United States Air Force!*

'*Duck!*' the guardsman screamed.

They fell into the snow.

Just in time. The bomb hit the bus which disappeared in a violent ball of yellow-red flame.

The twin-boom Lightning came tearing down out of the sky again. Violent lights crackled along its wings. A stream of red and white tracer hissed at the soldiers on the road. They broke and scattered over the field. Here and there a man dropped into the snow.

Another bomb wobbled down from beneath the Lightning's belly. Seconds later the truck exploded.

'Come on,' Crooke yelled with the last of his strength, 'get into the wood!'

The Yank got to his feet and blew an exuberant handkiss at the departing fighter-bomber. 'Whoever you are, brother, I love ya!'

High in the sky, the pilot did a triumphant victory-roll.

SECTION FOUR: OPERATION KILL

'It's carnival, *Reichsführer.* I always feel well at carnival time.'

Gruppenführer Anna Grossmann, head of OPERATION KILL, to Heinrich Himmler, March 1943.

1

'*Reichsführer* – you!' Anna Grossmann said hoarsely into the phone which Heidi had just handed her.

Heinrich Himmler, the one-time chicken farmer and now the most-feared man in Occupied Europe, answered in his somewhat pedantic voice. 'Yes, Grossmann – me. Heil Hitler!'

'Heil Hitler, *Reichsführer*,' she answered dutifully and winked at Heidi, whose pretty blue eyes were round with awe. It wasn't every day that one got to talk to the policeman who controlled Europe from the Channel to German-occupied Russia. 'And how are you?'

Far away in Berlin, Himmler cleared his throat. 'Well, thank you, Grossmann,' he said. 'But as you can imagine – up to my neck in work. The Führer wants me to raise four new *Waffen SS* divisions for the summer offensive...' Suddenly Himmler remembered his manners; at heart he was a very conventional, bourgeois person. 'But how are you, Grossmann? Keeping well, I hope?'

The tall, thin woman laughed shortly. 'It's carnival, *Reichsführer*. I always feel well at carnival time, although we have not been allowed to celebrate *officially* since the war.'

Himmler gave a polite chuckle. Anna Grossmann could imagine him fiddling with his pince-nez. 'Ah you Rhinelanders – nothing in your heads but celebrating at this time of the year!'

'Yes,' Anna Grossmann said, and reached out her hand so that Heidi could take it in hers. 'Down here we celebrate the feasts as they fall, you know.' She knew that she could afford the little joke. The *Reichsführer* was a completely humourless man, but his mistress-secretary was from the Rhineland herself, and she and Hedwig had been good friends before she had left Cologne to move into the love-nest Himmler had built for her.

'Apparently,' Himmler commented drily. He raised his voice. 'Now, Grossmann, what is the situation with Operation Kill? Schellenberg informed me this morning that his agents in London report the Russians are putting pressure on Anglo-Americans to invade the Continent this summer. I should like to be able to report to the Führer at my next audience that Operation Kill is ready to be put into practice as soon as the first invader places his foot on French soil. Please fill me in.'

Anna could hear the second handpiece of the scrambler being picked up. That would be one of Himmler's aides, ready to jot down notes on their conversation.

She waited a second to let him get ready, idly stroking Heidi's hand and wondering how reliable Schellenberg's information was. Then she began, proud of her photographic memory for figures. 'At present we have some 205,000 Anglo-Americans in our cages. Of these there are 52,000 British officers up to the rank of brigadier and some 10,000 American up to the rank of major–' She hesitated. 'I haven't got further with the *Ami* count because we've had a little trouble down here.'

'Trouble?' Himmler snapped. Anna Grossmann grinned at Heidi. She could well imagine the *Reichsführer* frowning over his pince-nez. It was a look that might frighten Nebe, Schellenberg, Kaltenbrunner and the rest; but it didn't frighten her.

'Yes,' she said. 'Six Tommies escaped from Stalag Luft VIIb after killing one of my people.'

'What have you done about it?'

'They are being taken care of *Reichsführer*,' she answered, in no way disturbed by his outrage. She knew her '*Reichsheini*'; he was as tame as a lamb in the right hands, and fearful of his own shadow to boot. In the good old days in Berlin before the war, Heydrich had told her a lot about Himmler during their frequent drunken carousals in Salon Kitty.

'On H-Day – or immediately before it,' she continued, 'if Schellenberg or Canaris can warn us in time – we assemble the first batch of a thousand in Cologne. I've picked the city, not because it's my birthplace, but because it will make a suitably bombed background.'

'I see.'

'We'll execute them publicly – one hundred at a time – by firing squads.'

'And the foreign Press?'

'I have already been in touch with Minister von Ribbentrop. He assures me that his people can have selected representatives of the neutral Press – Swedes, Swiss and the like – at Cologne-Wahn airport within two hours of receiving the word from me. But naturally our own Cologne radio people will be present to give – if you forgive the pun,

Reichsführer – a blow by blow account to the world.' While she waited for Himmler's answer, she pursed her lips and blew Heidi a kiss. The pretty teenager in the uniform of a *Blitzmadchen** moved back a little, the smile disappearing from her face. Anna reached for a little bottle of cheap scent with her free hand. Heidi caught her look and the movement. She placed her hand in Anna's pocket and gave her it. Hastily the older woman splashed its contents over the front of her neat uniform tunic. Himmler spoke again. 'That sounds good to me, Grossmann. One thing, however. I am not so confident in the abilities of those gentlemen in the Wilhelmstrasse.' He was referring to Ribbentrop's Foreign Ministry. 'It would not be the first time that those same fine gentlemen have made a mess of things. I suggest that you make your own arrangements through the Reich Main Security Office in Berlin to have them supply the plane to transport the foreign newsmen to Cologne when H-Day arrives.'

'*Einverstanden, Reichsführer,*' she snapped in her best imitation of her male colleagues.

*The German equivalent of the wartime British ATS.

'That is a good suggestion.'

'I think so,' Himmler replied. 'Now, I must get back to those divisions. Heil Hitler!'

'Heil Hitler, *Reichsführer,*' she answered.

The phone went dead.

For a moment she held it in her hand. Then she winked again and hugged Heidi.

'Is he going to come?' Heidi asked anxously.

'No, thank God. You know what a terrible middle-class prude he is,' Grossmann said happily. 'He's going to leave the whole of Operation Kill to me. And do you know what we're going to do, Heidi? We're going to have a party!'

'A party!' Heidi exclaimed. 'To celebrate Carnival?'

Anna Grossmann chuckled. As she did so, she could hear her ravaged lungs wheeze, but this day she had no time for her disease; she would worry about that *after* the Carnival was over. 'Of course, what would life be for a good Rhinelander without it?'

Heidi clapped her hands like a little girl. 'When?'

'When else but Rose Monday. But of course, it must not come out. The Führer has forbidden all such festivities since Stalingrad, as you know?'

Heidi knew. Her only brother had gone into Russian captivity with the rest of von Paulus's staff. God only knew whether he were still alive! 'But who shall we invite?'

Grossmann stared up at the high barrelled roof of the castle's medieval entrance hall, decorated with the faded flags of the long-dead von Totenbergs, whose home this had been before Schloss Totenberg had become her headquarters.

'I know,' she said, 'all the people who are involved in Operation Kill. We could use it as a cover if anything leaked out. We'll have a Carnival conference, eh?'

'Excellent!' Heidi breathed in admiration. 'You are so clever!'

'You flatter me,' Anna said. 'Yes, we'll invite Doerr and Viktor – and that little *Haupsturmführer* who keeps making eyes at you.'

Heidi blushed. 'Oh, don't be so foolish, Anna,' she said. 'You know that you are the only one I love.' To emphasize her words, she stood on tiptoe and pressed her lips to those of the older woman lovingly. They clung together in silence.

Three hundred yards away, well covered by the thick gorse, Crooke lowered the Dutchman's high-powered field glass. 'Okay, Piet,' he whispered, taking his eyes off the castle perched on the crag opposite, 'let's move out.'

Piet Straat nodded. He pulled the metal stock off the Sten, which he had kept at the ready all the time Crooke had been watching the castle, and stuck it under his loose jacket. Crooke concealed the other two parts. 'Not too much noise,' Crooke warned as the Dutchman began to move down the steep incline. 'We don't want to be caught out now.'

The Lightning's surprise attack had given the Destroyers a head start. By the time the surviving soldiers had contacted the nearest authorities, they were deep in the forest. All day long the spotter planes droned over their heads and far away they could hear the searchers' vehicles racing up and down the forest tracks. But neither the planes nor the searchers had really impeded their escape; the firs offered ideal cover.

Crooke had taken a calculated risk in not turning due west. He reasoned that the enemy would expect them to swim the Moselle, only a few kilometres away to the west, and across into occupied Luxembourg, where they might expect to find friends. Instead he had marched due north inside Germany, moving parallel to the frontier. The Eifel woods had provided good cover virtually all the way and by the time it had grown dark on that first day they had swung round Trier and were camped safely in a wood on the road to Bitburg.

On the night of the second day they had waded through the River Sauer which marked Germany's border with the northern tip of Luxembourg and had found a friendly farmer who offered them a meal of bread and cheese, his barn to hide in for the day and the advice to 'watch out for those folk in the East Cantons'.

When he had gone away, Thaelmann explained that he had meant the people of the two eastern provinces of Belgium, St Vith and Eupen, which had been German up to 1919 and were now German again. In spite of the warning Crooke decided to cross the well-wooded area, because his men were weakening and it was the most direct route to the *Dreilaendereck* where he hoped to contact the Dutch partisans. During the next two days they wandered through the Ardennes, losing and finding themselves repeatedly, living off milk, stolen from the churns placed at the roadside for collection, and turnips dug from the farmers' fields. For two whole days they did not see a soul, but by the end they were safely through the two eastern provinces and their goal was only a matter of miles away.

At the steep border village of Gemmenich they finally contacted the partisans. Just after dawn they posted themselves in the woods overlooking the single cobbled village street and examined the little red-bricked houses for any sign of life. Crooke's plan was to move through the place before anyone was awake and be over the border into Holland by the quickest route. Only the soft cooing of pigeons broke the stillness of the dawn. Stevens licked his lips hungrily. 'Could just do with a slice of pigeon pie now,' he said longingly.

'Be quiet!' Crooke said, but his mind was racing. Who would dare keep pigeons in occupied Belgium? He knew the Belgians were noted as pigeon fanciers, but surely in wartime and at the border with Nazi Germany...

'I think we've found them,' he said.

Half an hour later he was proved right. The little man who was hiding the carrier pigeons, dropped the year before, it later turned out, by SOE, nearly had a heart attack when they burst into the back kitchen. For one moment he took them for the local 'Order Police', Nazi collaborators to a man, but Crooke's halting German and subsequent English soon convinced him otherwise and he set off at once on his ancient bicycle with Thaelmann at his side to find the 'chief'.

Thereafter things happened quickly. Two hours later an ancient wood-burning Citroën carried them over the frontier. Near Aachen their silent, Sten-carrying guards hurried them into a little tumbledown half-timbered barn where Piet Straat began their interrogation.

Finally they were left to sleep the rest of the day, being shaken awake roughly in the middle of the night by an excited flushed Piet Straat, a bottle of *genever* in his hand and seven glasses.

'We have heard from London,' he had explained. 'You are all right. A Mister Mallory has vouched for you. He says welcome back to the bad pennies.' Piet had shrugged. 'Whatever that may mean – code I suppose.'

Over the next few days the messages went

back and forth from the radio concealed in Straat's tailor-shop in nearby Maastricht. Whatever Crooke might have thought privately of the elegant Naval Intelligence man, Mallory was certainly swift when it came to answering queries and requests for help.

The reply to his query about the mysterious Gestapo woman came back within twenty-four hours, courtesy the Dutch section of the SOE and the Allied War Crimes Section, War Office. 'Grossmann, Anna. B. 1900 Cologne. Trained teacher. Joined NSDAP* 1931. Became full-time official of the female 'Beauty and Belief' movement 1934. Transferred to the *Geheim Staatspolizei*** 1936. Taken up by Heydrich, head of the Reichs Security Main Office, Berlin 1939. Head of the regional Gestapo set-up attached to Wehrmacht Military District VI (Rhineland) 1942. HQ Schloss Totenberg. Present duties unknown.'

'Schloss Totenberg?' Piet exclaimed when Crooke asked him if he knew it. 'Of course,

* *National Sozialistische Deutsche Arbeiterpartei* i.e. Nazi Party.
** Full title of the Gestapo.

it is a showpiece of the Eifel. Only twenty minutes from here by car.'

'But what do they mean by present duties unknown, sir?' Stevens asked.

'Can't you guess? The murder of our boys in Jerry POW camps.'

Two days later Piet and Crooke joined the flood of Dutch and Belgian workers who crossed the border at Vaals every day to work in Aachen's booming war industries. At one stage the little blue and white tram was stopped and a fat middle-aged Schupo popped his head through the door to be greeted by a roar of obscene remarks from the 'Dutch' and 'Belgians' who spoke the same German dialect as he did.

Ten minutes later they were pedalling up the hill that led out of the city on the road that led to Monschau. Totenberg is situated on one of the Eifel's volcanic hills, its high pointed Gothic towers dominating the valleys around, as they have done for over five hundred turbulent years. 'You see,' Piet explained as they crouched in the gorse surveying it, 'this area is like an accordion. When the Germans are powerful, they expand outwards. When the French are powerful, they do the same.' He shrugged. 'And we border folk always get caught in the

273

squeeze, regardless of what side was putting on the pressure.'

Crooke smiled sympathetically. From his studies at Sandhurst he knew something of the border with its classic routes for invading armies – the Belfort, Metz and Losheim gaps – moving east or westwards.

The castle was a typical medieval defensive structure, its central keep built over the well and dominating the rest of the building in case the enemy ever managed to penetrate the outer walls – a highly unlikely event since the outer walls rose perpendicularly for some seventy feet. But that wasn't all. The medieval mason had copied a trick from the Saracens. He had curved the battlements outwards at an angle of forty degrees so that even if the enemy managed to get a scaling ladder in position under the wall, his attempts to get any farther would be made virtually impossible by the curve.

'One would need to be an alpinist to get up there, even today,' Piet commented.

'Yes,' Crooke agreed. 'The only way in is the obvious one.'

'What do you mean – the obvious one?'

'Through the front gate.'

'No,' Piet said decisively. 'That's not the way. A single recruit with a machine-gun

274

could hold up a regiment at that gate. It's only big enough for one vehicle or three men abreast. There's got to be another way.'

Crooke changed the subject slightly. 'Piet, have you any men locally?'

Piet looked at him a little bewildered. The tailor was not used to swift mental jumps. 'Yes, I do. There's a small colony of Dutch farm labourers in a camp between here and Monschau. They're allowed home on leave once a month. Sometimes they have odd bits of information for us.'

'Do you think that you could get one of them to survey this place every day and let us know what's going on – daily?' Piet made a rolling gesture with his thumb and forefinger. Crooke had been long enough in Nazi Germany to know what that meant – the oil which greased the wheels of progress – money.

'I'm sure Commander Mallory can take care of that one, but how are we going to get a daily report.'

Piet pointed to the buzzard hovering high above the grey castle in the harsh blue winter sky.

Crooke nodded. 'Oh, yes,' he said. 'The pigeons, of course.'

Thereafter the messages came in daily to the little concealed pigeon loft in Gemmenich. Scrawled in an illiterate hand, they were disappointing.

'Two trucks and a van entered today' ... 'Saw AG and secretary on ramparts this afternoon.' Twice the single word 'Nothing'. And then on the fifth day a long message scribbled on the thin rice paper.

'Nothing from T. In M. shopkeepers say big orders from T. Wine, schnaps, beer. Reason: On Rose Monday AG to celebrate Carnival.'

'M?' Crooke queried, passing the paper back to Piet, who set fire to it as a matter of routine.

'Monschau,' Piet explained. 'The Dutch workers go down there once a week on pay day to buy odds and ends.' He laughed softly. 'Mostly stuff the Nazis have looted from Holland.'

'I see,' Crooke said. 'And what's this Rose Monday and Carnival business?'

'It's a long story,' Piet said, as if he were preparing for an hour-long lecture.

'Please make it short.'

'All right. Well the Romans introduced a festival into this area of Europe – a pre-lenten celebration. It died out in the 17th century, but was revived in Cologne in 1820.'

'But what is it?' Crooke interrupted.

'A sort of springtime festival. Lots of drinking, dancing and–' He made another gesture with which Crooke had become familiar since he had arrived in Germany: a stiff forefinger poked back and forth through a hole made by the forefinger and thumb of the other hand.

'But the highpoint is what we call the "three crazy days". The three last days of the Carnival before Ash Wednesday, with Rose Monday being the most important. At least before the war. Hitler doesn't like people to enjoy themselves. Of course,' he shrugged, 'everyone knows why – he's impotent.'

Crooke nodded, and added the comment about Hitler's sexual ability to the rest of the legends he had already heard about the Führer in these last few days. 'But what form does this – er – Rose Monday take?'

The tailor stroked his long thin nose. 'What can I say? People go out on the streets and dance–'

'In March?'

Piet laughed. 'Sure. I've seen them out there half naked in temperatures way below zero and snowing like hell. You don't know the Rhinelanders and their temperament!'

'Half naked?' Crooke queried.

'Of course. Everyone dresses up. Masks and fancy costumes. In pre-war times, I used to make more money in January and February sewing costumes for the carnivalists than I did the rest of the year together.'

'Costumes?' Crooke said thoughtfully. 'Costumes.' He pulled at the patch, which the Moonlight Squadron Lysander had dropped the night before with their new weapons and the message from Mallory, beginning 'Admiral Godfrey sends his regards and hopes that the patch will serve to remind you of Nelson's motto and lend your hand new cunning and the "Nelson Touch".'

'Of course,' he said suddenly. 'That would be the "Nelson Touch"! Piet, I want you to do something for me!' And he began to explain his plan to the Dutchman whose eyes grew rounder and rounder, as Crooke listed the details.

2

'Schloss Totenberg!' Crooke announced, as they breasted the hill and lay panting in the snow staring at the Gothic towers sparkling in the moonlight. 'The Castle of Dead Man's Mountain,' Thaelmann translated. 'An apt name for those fascists who inhabit it.'

Down below the guards, armed with machine pistols, stopped another sleek black official Mercedes, packed with high ranking Gestapo men and their mistresses. The guards checked it thoroughly, even opening the boot. The sergeant in charge waved and the Mercedes drew away. It slid into the narrow entrance to the castle and disappeared.

'You see,' Crooke broke the silence in which they had studied the Mercedes, 'there's no chance of getting into the place that way.' He pointed to a spot high up on the castle wall away to the left of the gateway. 'At two o'clock – that window.'

Yank spotted it first. In spite of being the

279

oldest Destroyer, he had the keenest eyesight. 'I'm with you,' he said. It was a small barred window about three feet square.

Gippo was shivering in his thin silk Harlequin costume, made for him like the rest of their costumes by Piet and his apprentices. But in spite of his chattering teeth and almost blue face, his words were bold enough. 'We British chaps are not being afraid of such things,' he retorted. 'For me that is nothing.'

'Yer,' Stevens commented dourly, 'I'd bet half a nicker to a tanner that you've had plenty o' practice climbing in through windows, your horrible wog.'

'Are you saying that I am a–' Gippo began.

Crooke cut him short. 'That's enough, Gippo! We all know how brave you are. Come on, let's go.'

Gippo got to his feet and picked up his big pistol. The others followed, Stens at the ready. Silently they began to descend the steep slope towards Schloss Totenberg.

Under the revolving lights in the ceiling, which lit up their sweating excited drunken faces in vivid green, red and blue hues, the men and women of Operation Kill swayed back and forth in densely packed motion to the brassy music of the Brandenburger band, 'borrowed' from the Regiment's depot at near-by Dueren. The noise and heat were terrific. Sweat poured in streams from below the dancers' masks and to make themselves heard they were forced to shout at the tops of their voices.

The scene was macabre – a last frantic outburst of a doomed society: jockeys, harem girls, devils, cowboys, gauchos, ballerinas, dramatized by the vivid whirling hues, dancing their way to their deaths.

Obersturmbannführer Doerr, dressed as a 19th-century Prussian policeman complete with heavy curved moustache, sword and *Pickelhaube*, took one sticky hand off the naked back of his plump partner and nudged Viktor, his usually brick-red face now crimson with drink and excitement. 'Thou,' he panted, cupping his hand above the roar, 'let's have a drink!'

'Yes, *Obersturm–*' Viktor caught himself in time. 'Let us do that, *thou.*' During Carnival, everybody could be addressed in the familiar form, even one's boss. Viktor nudged his girl and together the four of them fought their way towards the great table that ran the length of the room. It was piled high with delicacies long since unobtainable in Nazi Germany: steaming sausages next to mounds of potato salads, smoked salmon and dishes of salt herrings, the old Carnival recipe for a hangover, huge dark-brown Ardennes hams from just over the border. But it was the centrepiece of the huge buffet which caught their attention.

Doerr's girlfriend gasped in admiration. 'Isn't it beautiful!' she simpered, staring up at the massive cake that towered above her blonde head.

Doerr squeezed her fat breast, his face flushed with champagne, dancing and the thought of her in bed later that night. 'But not as beautiful as you, my little cheetah!'

She giggled and tried to push away his big importuning fingers from her breast. 'Oh stop it, Walther,' she cried, her face flushed with excitement. 'Tell me what the word on the top of the cake means.'

For the first time Doerr saw the word, worked in red letters on the gleaming white of the cake's icing. It was difficult to read. Obviously the pastry cook had devoted great effort to forming its flying arabesques. With difficulty he spelled out the letters 'K-I-L-L.'

While Peters and the Yank took up covering positions, Stens at the ready, Gippo handed the big clumsy pistol to Crooke.

Half a dozen yards away the snow sparkled brightly in the moonlight and it was as bright as day. But here in the shadow of the great wall, they were hidden by the darkness. 'Okay,' he whispered, 'stand by.'

He walked back a few paces so that he could see the tiny window, way up above him. He licked his lips and hoped the SOE and Mallory had been right about the pistol's capabilities. Taking aim he pressed the trigger. A sharp crack. A tiny speck of flame darted from the muzzle followed by the grapnel. He felt the tug of the thin silk rope as it shot out. Hastily he stiffened his arm, with the pistol still raised high above his head. The rope flew straight into the night sky. It paused at the top of its parabola. A brief glimpse of the four-pronged grapnel. A split second later came the clang of metal against metal. Then all was silence.

Crooke held his breath. Had the German guards heard the clang? For what seemed ages the Destroyers froze in their action positions. But there was no shout or sudden crack of machine pistol from the front of the castle. Mallory had been right. The new Commando scaling pistol, still on the secret list, was virtually noiseless. Crooke breathed a sigh of relief and then put his whole weight on the rope. 'Gippo,' he hissed, 'you're on!'

Gippo hurried forward. He stuck the long knife into the pocket of his baggy silken pants and grasped the rope. He tested it and began to climb. Swiftly he shinned up the side of the castle, disappearing into the gloom.

'Just look at that,' Stevens whispered in mock awe. 'Didn't I always say them bloody wogs were half monkeys!'

Crooke had no time for Stevens' special brand of humour. His eyes were fixed on the dark shape clinging to the rope forty feet above their heads. He could not see the half-breed's movements, but he could imagine him letting his legs take the strain while his hands pulled out the stopper of the precious bottle, which the Lysander from the Moonlight Squadron had flown in the night before together with the scaling pistol.

The bottle was another one of the SOE's special little preparations, created for them in 'Winston Churchill's Toyshop,' as they called the research centre run by Colonel

Stuart Macrea at which such specialities as horse manure which turned out to be mines and lumps of coal that were bombs were manufactured. According to Mallory, the liquid contained in the bottle would loosen cement and mortar to a depth of two inches within thirty seconds.

Anxiously, Crooke waited to hear whether Mallory was right about the second gadget. There was a scraping of metal on stone. The rope began to move violently; obviously Gippo was wrenching the iron grill away from the little window. A soft cautious voice calling, 'Watch out below', confirmed it a moment later. The grill flew in an arc above their upturned heads and landed softly in the deep snow.

'All right, lads,' Crooke ordered, 'let's get on with it.'

Above them they heard the tinkle of breaking glass.

Then one by one they hauled themselves up the side of the castle.

The final act had begun.

Anna Grossmann waited at the head of the stairs, overlooking the throng of dancers below, swaying in packed intimacy to the music of the Brandenburgers. She was happy. The Carnival celebration was going splendidly. Now she was ready to make her entrance, but as usual Heidi had not yet finished dressing.

As she stared down at the men and women below, all of whom were initiated into the great secret which might yet win the war for the Fatherland, she reflected on how far she had come in the past ten years. It had been a long hard fight, for the Party hierarchy was bourgeois and imbued with the old anti-female philosophy of the woman's place being at the stove – *children, kitchen, cooking:* that's all they knew. But her father, whom she had loved deeply, had taught her to be hard when he had learned that her mother had bequeathed the scourge of TB to his daughter. Now at last she was in charge, the boss of all the women – and men – enjoying her hospitality below.

'I'm ready, darling.'

She turned, startled out of her reverie.

Heidi was dressed in the costume of the twenties: a shimmering tight silken sheath, its fringed hem well above her black stockinged knees, its neck plunging to reveal a firm bosom, which needed no bra to hold it up.

'You look lovely, darling.' Bending gravely in an unconscious parody of her long-dead father, she touched her dry lips to the girl's hand. *'Kuss die Hand, Gnaediges Fraulein,'* she murmured.

Heidi caught her giggle just in time. It would never do to offend Anna when she was playing her male role.

With that carefully faked affection, which had fooled Anna for so long, she lifted the Gestapo chief's head.

'But what about you?' she said merrily. 'Now that's what I call a costume!'

Heidi looked at the tight black jacket, the striped pants, the high wing collar and spats, which made up Anna's costume and again barely restrained herself from laughing.

'It's a terrific outfit,' she said enthusiastically. 'Where did you get it?'

'It was my dear father's,' Anna said proudly. She held out her arm in grave old-world courtesy. 'But come on, gracious miss, let's not keep our guests waiting.' She ran her hand through her sleek grey hair and then thrust it in her pocket. Together they began to descend the great stone staircase. From the rostrum the bandmaster spotted them. He raised his hands and the musicians stopped in the middle of their waltz. Energetically the bandmaster brought his hands down again. The rattle of brass drew the guests' eyes to the staircase. There was a hush as they caught sight of the man who wasn't a man and the girl who was no virgin, but who had never known a man. Heads bent together. Whispers broke out everywhere. Anna ignored them. Gravely she swept down the stairs while Heidi tripped at her side. Doerr, a knowing grin on his drunken face, nudged Viktor. Together they began to applaud. Gradually their clapping was taken up by the others. Anna bent her head in gracious acknowledgement, a monarch deigning to notice his subjects. She spoke to the bandmaster. He turned to his band again. 'One, two, three,' he commanded, tapping his foot. With military élan, the Brandenburgers launched into a Strauss waltz. Still clapping, the guests stepped back to allow Anna and 'her' Heidi to begin their solo dance. As Anna launched awkwardly into the waltz, those in the know could see the bulge in the front of her tight striped pants. And they knew what that was.

One by one the Destroyers flitted down the dark corridor, their footsteps muffled by the thick socks they had put on over their shoes. Cautiously Crooke opened the door at the end. Nothing save another long corridor and in the distance the muffled sound of dance music. 'Come on,' he said. They pushed on down the passage, lit by naked bulbs, their weak yellow light throwing their shadows into gigantic relief. The music was louder now. Crooke opened another door and this time the blast of music hit them full in the face. Hurriedly Crooke shut it again. 'We're there, lads,' he said. 'Put your masks on as soon as we are through the door. Leave the woman to me – I'll take care of her.' He turned to Thaelmann, who appropriately enough wore the striped suit of a 19th-century convict. 'You can come with me and give me fire-cover. The rest of you spread yourselves around the balcony. Look here.' Carefully he opened the door to indicate where they should take up their positions.

'You take the head of the stairs, Yank...'

He stopped short.

A tall slim man was standing in the gloom of the balcony, only a matter of feet away, staring at them, his mouth open in drunken surprise!

He was dressed in a blood-stained white apron and a blue-and-white striped jacket such as is customarily worn by German butchers. To complete the costume, in his hand he held an enormous wooden cleaver, also painted red.

'You!' he breathed, raising it slowly. *'Crooke!'*

'Jesus H,' the Yank said over Crooke's shoulder, reacting first. 'It's that Kraut sawbones!'

'Winkler!' Crooke hissed, raising his Sten.

'Butcher Winkler,' the SS doctor said. 'Death, I presume?' he nodded at Crooke's vivid black and white skeleton costume.

'You knew all the time,' Crooke stuttered. 'Those symptoms of yours … they were fake! You knew about her all along.'

Winkler smiled drunkenly. 'Naturally. The bitch believes she rules the world. One has to show her that she doesn't. And now death has come to fetch her, eh?'

'You're drunk,' was all that Crooke could manage to get out, shocked both by Winkler's revelation and his treachery to the woman who was his boss. What boundless self-hatred must have gone into his decision to tell Crooke as soon as he realised that the woman he was seeking was none other that Anna Grossmann!

'Blau wie ein Veilchen!' Winkler said drunkenly, a stupid smile on his pale face.

'As blue as a violet – the German phrase has it.' He stood there swaying, his hand still held out, as if to take Crooke's.

'Don't be a damn fool, Winkler! Stop that stupid chatter and come in here. You'll be safe, I promise you.' He made a grab for the doctor.

With surprising agility, Winkler darted back out of reach. Now he was full in view of anyone standing below and looking up. 'Death must shake hands with the butcher,' he said thickly. 'We're in the same trade, aren't we?'

'Winkler,' Crooke said desperately, 'you don't need to die.' But even as he said the words, he knew that he must. Indeed he wanted to die. Self-revulsion was written all over him.

Even as he spoke in one last vain attempt to save the doctor, Gippo acted. He drew the knife from his pocket and threw it. It caught Winkler in the chest. He gave a long, high scream. Slowly he began to tilt over the balcony. With one last cry he fell backwards. A lamp interrupted his fall. It splintered and crashed to the floor, followed by the heavy thud of his body.

'We're for it now!' Stevens yelled.

'Quick!' Crooke ordered.

They piled through the door. Down below the music had faltered and died away. In horror the guests stared at the figure sprawled in a star of red blood in the centre of the floor. They seemed mesmerised by it as the Destroyers rushed into the kill. A red-faced man in the blue uniform of a Prussian gendarme was the first to react. He looked up at the balcony and pulled out a pistol. It wasn't a dummy: it was the real thing.

'Doerr – the bastard!' Stevens screamed.

Bullets zipped through the air. Slivers of wood from the panels behind them spattered around Crooke's head. He ducked and let loose a burst. It missed Doerr, but sent men and women to both sides of him skidding to the floor. Pandemonium broke out. Screams went up on all sides as the guests scampered for cover. At Crooke's side, Stevens did not let himself be put off his aim. His Sten gun rattled, deafening the officer.

Doerr's legs buckled. The gun tumbled from his fingers. But his momentum carried him forward. Head first he crashed into a gigantic bowl of punch.

Crooke swung down the stairs three at a time trying to find Anna Grossmann in the confusion of the screaming guests. Cracks of blue flame and the lead singing through the air indicated that Doerr was not the only one armed. But Crooke ignored the bullets. Time was of the essence. The guards would soon hear the shooting and come running to investigate.

On the balcony the Stens of the others were sawing huge paths of death through the guests; the Destroyers could not miss. It was a massacre – a cold-blooded massacre. A heavy-set man, dressed absurdly in a German clippie's peaked cap and short blue skirt, lifted it up to reveal hairy unshaven legs, as he grabbed frantically for a pistol. His fingers had just closed on it and pulled it out, when Crooke's burst caught him in his stomach and he fell dead.

Suddenly a well-remembered face loomed up in the midst of the blood-bath. The man was dressed in gaudy gaucho's clothes. It was Viktor with a pistol in his hand. Crooke remembered the bathroom in Trier, the horror of that little white-tiled room. He pressed the Sten's trigger but no answering chatter came. He had emptied the mag already! Feverishly he yanked it out and grabbed for the spare in his secret pocket.

Viktor grinned. 'You,' he said. Almost deliberately he raised his pistol, clasping it in both hands for steadiness, as if he had all the time in the world. 'All right, Mr Death, meet...'

He never finished. The Yank let him have a full burst at twenty yards range which took the top of his head clean off.

The firing was ebbing away now. Some of the guests remained standing. The air was filled with the cries of the dying among the bodies of those already dead. A long way off there was the clatter of the guards' heavy boots up the stone flags of the main gate. But Thaelmann was already placing the cunning little mines which Mallory called 'de-bollockers'. 'You'll live after one of them hits you in the groin,' the SOE instructor had explained. 'But you'll never be much good in bed afterwards.'

Desperately Crooke looked round for Anna Grossman. The sound of running feet was getting louder when at last he spotted her crouching behind the great cake, holding a sobbing girl in her arms. 'Anna Grossmann?' he cried above the chatter of the Stens.

Slowly, almost calmly, she turned her head in Crooke's direction. There was no sign of fear on her pale emaciated face. She patted the terrified girl's hand reassuringly.

'There, there,' she said soothingly. 'It's only death.' She coughed. 'An insignificant man in death's clothes.'

Crooke did not understand the words, but he could recognize the boundless contempt for the male in her eyes. He thought of the young pilot officer in England, the pile of white ashes in the camp, the walking striped-pyjama skeletons of the outer compound. Calmly with almost clinical detachment he pressed the trigger of the Sten. Anna Grossmann screamed. With her arms cradled around the already dead girl, she sank to the floor, dragging Heidi with her in one last embrace. An instant later she was dead herself.

The firing had stopped but Crooke remained motionless. In the past few years he had killed many men, gunning them down in the heat of battle or when – as that fine empty military phrase had it – 'the situation warranted it'. Now for the first time he had slaughtered a woman in cold blood. He stared down at his victims.

Anna Grossmann was spread-eagled on her back, her ugly yellow false teeth bulging from her mouth. Across her emaciated bony face the striped tie which had once belonged to her father lay like a squashed adder. Her one hand was concealed under the girl's body whose skirt had ridden up her legs. Her other was outstretched, palm outwards, to reveal a cheap bottle of scent. Slowly Crooke bent and smoothed the dead girl's skirt. He straightened up again and pulled out the metal identity discs which they had been given on their arrival at Stalag VIIb.

Deliberately he flipped them one after the other onto the woman's chest intoning their names monotonously. 'Crooke ... Thaelmann ... Jones ... Peters ... Gippo ... Stevens...' Then Peters grabbed his arm and shook him out of his reverie and they began to pelt back together the way they had come. Behind them at the great door the first agonizing screams indicated that the cruel little mines were holding the guards at bay. Crooke knew that the thugs of the Gestapo would never dare hurt some poor unfortunate Allied 'Kriegie' again.

The six metal discs on the dead body of Anna Grossmann would ensure that.

3

The silence of the night was disturbed by a faint buzzing sound. As the partisans prepared to rush out into the field and illuminate the signal, Piet, crouched next to Crooke, cocked his head to the wind and grunted: 'It's them, all right.'

With two other men he ran into the centre of the field, where torches were fixed to three sticks shaped in the form of an 'L'. He flicked the red signal light on and off twice.

The dark shape, circling above their head at about four hundred feet, replied by two brief red flashes. Now Crooke and the rest of the Destroyers, waiting in the undergrowth, knew that things would move swiftly. A pick-up op relied very much on split-second timing. The two light planes ended their circle. Flying against the wind they came down along the long arm of the now illuminated 'L'. The first Lysander hit the field with a squeal of protesting rubber. A moment later the second followed. Their engines racing, making enough noise, it seemed to the Destroyers, to wake the whole of Holland, they taxied along the shorter arm of the 'L'. Finally they came to a stop with the wind behind them in case they had to make an emergency start, a not too infrequent occurrence for the daring pilots of the SOE's Moonlight Squadron.

Piet cupped his hands around his mouth and yelled 'Come on!' The Destroyers needed no urging. They ran across to the waiting aircraft and moments later they were pumping the hand of the first young pilot, slapping him on the back and giving expression to their relief that they were getting out of Occupied Europe with a whole skin.

'Hello, so the bad pennies turn up again,' a familiar voice said, as the second pilot strolled across to them, as if he had all the time in the world and the Gestapo was on another planet.

'Commander Mallory!' Stevens gasped.

Mallory pulled off his leather flying helmet. 'Flight Lieutenant Wells to you, Stevens,' he said firmly. 'Admiral Godfrey doesn't know I'm on this op. If he did, he'd have my guts for garters.'

The next moment they were shaking his hand and slapping him on the back too, ignoring his rank and his well-bred reserve which frowned upon such familiarity. 'Come on now,' he said, 'I thought my Destroyers were strong silent men, not given to excess of emotion.'

'At this moment, sir,' Stevens chortled, 'you look better than Rita Hayworth to me!'

'I'm flattered,' Mallory replied.

Quickly while the Destroyers unloaded a new consignment of arms Crooke and Mallory exchanged a few words, shouted against the roar of the engines. 'The German papers from Aachen reported 56 dead and 37 seriously wounded at Schloss Totenberg in their yesterday issues,' Crooke yelled, cupping his hand so that Mallory could hear.

'Yes, and we intercepted a Gestapo message at Bletchley Park* two days ago in which Himmler queried why over the last week thirty-seven top officials had volunteered for frontline service.'

'One does not need a crystal ball to know why, Commander – er Flight Lieutenant. They obviously think they're in for a wave of

*At Bletchley, 50 miles north-west of London which housed the British top secret code-breaking and communications department.

assassinations. I have a feeling we won't have any more trouble.'

The unloading was finished. The Destroyers shook hands with Piet, who had tears in his eyes, and started to file into the little planes. Gippo got in first, clutching the loot he had taken from the bodies in the hall. Winkler's SS cufflinks alone would be worth a small fortune if he could find the right American officer. He'd tell the Yank they belonged to Himmler. Thaelmann followed, throwing a glance at the dark hilly horizon which was his homeland. If he felt anything at leaving it behind, his face showed nothing of his emotions. Stevens brought up the rear, his mind already in the London pubs with their easy female pickings. Perhaps this time he'd try the old officer and gentleman bit. After all he had been a temporary gentleman for the past few weeks – and officers always got the best birds.

'All right,' Mallory shouted against the noise, 'the other three of you are with me.'

'Yes, sir,' the guardsman snapped woodenly, unconsciously standing to attention. Even on a clandestine operation like this he could not forget his years of training with the Brigade. He got into the little canvas seat and sat in it bolt-upright, as if on parade.

As Crooke and the Yank followed, Mallory cried, 'And by the way, Crooke, the Bletchley wallahs also picked up a message from German Army HQ. It read. "Who or what are the Destroyers?"'

'Interesting.'

'But do you know who signed it?' Mallory cried, as he fumbled with the unfamiliar controls.

'No.'

'The Führer.'

If Mallory had expected some reaction, he did not get it. Crooke nodded. 'One day soon,' he said drily, 'the Führer will find out *who* or *what* the Destroyers are.'

The publishers hope that this book has given you enjoyable reading. Large Print Books are especially designed to be as easy to see and hold as possible. If you wish a complete list of our books please ask at your local library or write directly to:

Dales Large Print Books
Magna House, Long Preston,
Skipton, North Yorkshire.
BD23 4ND

This Large Print Book, for people
who cannot read normal print,
is published under the auspices of

THE ULVERSCROFT FOUNDATION